WANNA BE LOVED BY A BOSS

TINK RICHARDSON

Wanna Be Loved by A Boss

Copyright © 2019 by Tink Richardson

Published by Shan Presents
www.shanpresents.com

SYNOPSIS

Zoiena Sulton wants nothing more than to continue living her best life. She owns her own cafe, which she opened a year ago after her fathers death. On top of that, she hasn't dated since her last boyfriend broke up with her and left town.

Her only focus is herself and her bag. That is until she meets Cashmere "Cash" Logan, with his smooth talk, charming ways, and not to mention how he put it down in the bedroom.
But is all that enough to make Zoiena believe he won't hurt her?

Find out in this rollercoaster of a love story.

SUBSCRIBE

Text Shan to 22828 to stay up to date with new releases, sneak peeks, contest, and more....

SUBMISSIONS

To submit your manuscript to Shan Presents, please send the first
three chapters and synopsis to submissions@shanpresents.com

1

ZOIENA SULTON

Taking a sip from my Starbucks mocha latte, and a bite from my cream cheese bagel, I pulled up and parked my 2017 Acura near the street that was home to my business. *The Marigold Café* was something I was definitely proud of, and business was definitely booming. I hurried up and unlocked the door, so I could start preparing for the breakfast crowd.

"Well, it's about time you finally got here. I been waiting for a hour and a half out here." Said my friend Bianca. She worked at the café as my pastry chef, and she was the best there was. She could whip up a mean double chocolate cake, and her key lime pie was the best selling on our menu.

"Bianca, how has it been a hour and you literally just called me 20 minutes ago saying you just got here?"

"Well, it felt like a hour. You know I like to get here early to prepare for the lunch crowd. And then I have this huge order to do for a corporate event this weekend."

"Well, spend more time baking and less partying you would get it done," I joked. Bianca was the party animal out the two of us. I was more reserved and quiet.

"Whatever. Open up the door hoe."

I opened the door and turned on the lights. Within 25 minutes we had our first few regular customers walking in the door like they do every morning.

"Good morning ladies. Actually working I see," said my other best friend Triston, who worked as the cashier.

"Well, look whose actually on time today," Bianca teased.

"And look whose not hungover from a "long" night last night," Triston fires back. I swear these two are always at it.

"Well, at least I ain't got a messed up hairline. What the fuck? Ya barber blind," we both laughed.

"Well at least I'm not fucking mine."

"Hey! Will you two stop it before our customers hear you," I intervened.

"Don't blame me; he started it," Bianca said and went to the back to finish stirring her ingredients.

"You know I'm starting to think she like me, the way she always on my dick about stuff," Triston said.

"Not on ya life!" Bianca shouted from the back.

Me, Bianca, and Triston all went to the same high school together. Once I opened up my café they asked no questions about coming to work for me. Bianca thought it would be a good way to advertise her baking skills, which she inherited from her grandmother, and Triston pretty much did anything I asked of him. He was the best guy friend I had. If I needed to borrow money, he was there. If I needed a guy's advice, he was there. If I needed someone to go get a pedicure with, he would accompany me. Triston was the best.

"It's nothing wrong with your hairline Triston. You know Bianca is just teasing."

"I know it ain't shit wrong with my hairline. She better be more worried about her lace front not shedding in the cake batter." We both chuckled. I had to admit that was funny.

"Yeah, well thank you for being on time today Triston."

"No problem. Anything for you boss lady," He smiled at me.

I used to think Triston had it for me, but he never tried anything.

Sometimes when guys are friends with girls, eventually it leads to something else. With Triston it was different though. He never tried to kiss me, or try anything sexual so I just stopped thinking about it.

I walked to the back to see Bianca preparing a dozen chocolate Snicker cupcakes. I took out the pork roast in the fridge that I had marinating and set the oven to 450. It should be ready by lunch time.

"Don't think I ain't hear y'all say something about my wig. Y'all not funny."

"You and Triston need to quit."

"No, he need to quit with that hairline."

"His hairline isn't that messed up though Bianca."

"Girl please, you just saying that because that's your favorite best friend."

"Both of y'all are my favorite."

"Ok. Prove it," she said as she poured the cupcake batter into the pan.

"Prove it how?"

"Come out with me tonight to this party."

"Tonight?! Are you crazy? Do you know how much work I have to do today? I'm not going to be in no shape to go to someone's party."

"Oh, come on Zo; it's going to be lit. I even heard the Migos is going to be there."

"Bianca, who goes to a party in the middle of the week. It's only Wednesday."

"Umm, fun people." I understand I could be a little boring at times, but I be so busy with work, I don't have time to go out like that.

"And what am I suppose to wear? My flour dusted apron?"

"I got a extra outfit you can wear. You can come over my house after we close and pick something out."

"Uh uh, I am not wearing one of your "Hey come suck me down outfits" attracting too much attention."

"That's the point!"

"...I don't know. It's just been so long since I been out somewhere." Bianca put the tray in the oven and set the timer.

"Look, I know it was a tough year losing your dad and dealing with that loser ex-boyfriend of yours, but now is the time to let go and move on. Enjoy your life."

I gave some thought to what Bianca said. I have been kind of shut in when it comes to enjoying my life. When my father died, it took a lot of me. He actually taught me how to cook. Chef Reginald Sulton was the most famous Black chef in Los Angeles. He cooked for celebrities and famous politicians, traveled the world and cooked for people in other countries. He even got a invite to the royal palace in the UK and the White House. Three years ago, he got diagnosed with stage 4 prostate cancer, and last year unfortunately he lost the fight. Even though I know he was at peace, I missed him dearly.

Two months after that, my boyfriend who I was with for two years just randomly called me up and said he didn't want to be with me anymore. No explanation, no nothing. When I went by his house to talk things out, I was expecting to find him with another female, but instead I found nothing. His apartment was completely empty. The landlord told me he packed everything and moved out two days before that. Something about he was moving to New York or something, and whatever, what, or who was there has kept him there ever since. I was depressed for so long after that. I wouldn't eat, I didn't come out the house for four days, and Bianca and Triston had to literally almost break in for me to open the door.

Months went passed, and I started to feel regular again. Eventually, I saved up enough money to open up my own café with some dishes inspired by my dad. Good soul cooking and a bougie twist. As far as me dating, I talked to guys here and there but nothing more. After a while they would just stop answering the phone or stop texting. I know for sure my dad would want me to go out and have a good time.

"Ok fine. I'll go."

"Yay. I'm so excited. We going to have so much fun."

"Where is this place anyway?"

"It's up West Hollywood. Some Club called Zodiac."

"That new nightclub that just opened up?"

"Yeah, that's the one. Girl, all the fine ass ballers be going there."

I rolled my eyes. That was Bianca for you.

Later that day.....

We usually stay open until 5pm, but I closed down a little early today so I could go to Bianca's house and get ready. We counted the profit for today and locked the store down.

"So what time you hoes going be ready?" Asked Triston.

"Uhh, hold up, who said you was coming?" asked Bianca.

"Oh, so I can't come?"

"No. This is a girls' night out. Not girls plus one guy. How are we supposed to get any niggas phone number if you are with us," Bianca replied.

"Bianca, the niggas you mess with are short and broke, with no money. I'm starting to think that's your type."

"If only that wasn't ya momma type. Otherwise, you would be a lot more good looking," Bianca spat back.

"Whatever. I got plans any way."

"We promise to call when we get in later Triston."

"Ok," He smile quickly turned upside down.

We walked off in different directions. I left in Bianca's car and parked my car around back to leave it. Bianca's house was about 30 minutes away in Torrence. When we got there, I went through her closet and found a cute black mini dress with the back out and heels to match. I had my red Michael Kors purse, and pandora bracelet so I was pretty much set. I showered, flat ironed my hair, got dressed, and beat my face. Bianca wore a purple two-piece outfit, with some black red bottoms, and YSL purse.

Ready to go, we got back in the car, and drove up to West Hollywood. We parked and went to stand in line to get in.

"Girl, you see the bitches sweating me already. They know I'm ready to take any niggas they talk to tonight."

"Oh God, please don't get into a drunk fight tonight."

"Why not? Drunk fights are the best." I turned to get out of line. "I'm kidding, I'm kidding. I promise no drunk fights tonight."

"...*pick it up, then throw that shit down. Speed it up then slow that shit down, on the gang!*" After waiting in line for a half hour, we finally got into the packed club. The DJ was spinning "Thotiana" by Blueface. We went over to the bar and had our first shot of the night.

"I see a lot of good looking men up in here. Wonder which one I'm going to take home."

"How bout none of em. Do you know how many of these guys probably got diseases and stuff?"

"Uhh ok, can you turn off the grandma button, and turn on the turn up button."

"Ok. Fine. Maybe one more shot should do it."

"One?! Bitch, you need like five more shots."

We ordered some more shots of vodka, and finally went out on the dance floor. I was starting to feel good from the all the liquor, twerking to the music that was playing. Next thing I know when I turned around, Bianca was gone. I looked around the crowd but didn't see her anywhere. I instantly started to get paranoid, until I seen her over in the corner dancing on some buff looking guy with a nice wavy haircut.

"Your friend seems to really like my brother huh?" A voice whispered in my ear.

I turned around to see this tall light-skinned guy, with tattoos everywhere and short, curly hair standing behind me.

"Ummm, Yeah. She does," I said feeling real nervous. It wasn't that I didn't know how to talk to guys, but something about this nigga had me feeling like I had the inability to talk.

"Cash." He held out his hand.

"Zoiena," I shook it, hoping he couldn't feel me shaking.

"So Zoiena, would you like to share a dance with me?"

"All these big booty girls in here and you want to dance with me?"

"Yeah, it's a lot of big booty hoes in here. But how many of em look like you though?" I blushed. Who was this guy? Where did he come from?

"I should really go get my friend."

"Shiiid, ya friend look ight to me." I looked over to see her grinding all up on the guy she was with.

"Come on. I won't bite. If you don't want me to."

"..honestly I'm trying to stay focused, you must think I got to be joking"

Just as we headed back to the dance floor, the DJ started playing "Girls Need Love" by Summer Walker. Everyone started slow grinding on each other all over the club. With my alcohol set all the way in, I felt more looser. When I started dancing on this mystery guy, I instantly felt his dick getting hard. I didn't have your average stripper body with big titties and a fat ass, but I had some nice sized C-cup breasts, and a 32-inch waist, with a butt that poked out. I guess I was what you called slim thick.

Trying to not focus on this giant stick in the back of me, I continued to grind on it. And the more I did the harder it got. He put his head down in my neck; he had to bend down a little bit because he was so tall. At least 6'4.

"Baby girl, you ain't gotta play games with me. I know you feeling me."

"And how do you know that?"

"I'm a man. I can tell these things."

Feeling so tipsy at this point, I didn't even notice my hand went from my side, to accidentally touching his package a little bit. I immediately backed off him out of embarrassment. I turned to look at him thinking he would be mad, but he wasn't. He just had this small smirk on his face, like he was expecting me to do that.

"I'm sorry I.....You know what, maybe I should go," I turned to start to leave, but he grabbed my wrist and grabbed me around my torso, making my stomach touch his.

"You know if I can make you act this way from just dancing, imagine how I can make you feel in the bedroom."

Before I could even say anything, I heard a lot of noise coming from the corner where Bianca was. I turned around to look and see her clocking some girl in the face and having a full blown brawl. I tore away from Cash and ran over to pull her off the girl. After she finally let the girl hair go or more like detached her weave from her scalp, security started walking over.

"Come on, Bianca, let's go now!"

"No, no fuck this bitch! I ain't done stomping her face in yet."

I grabbed her arm and we headed for the exit. We got to her car, with her in the passenger seat because she was obviously too fucked up to drive, and we peeled out the parking lot.

"What the hell Bianca?! What was that all about?"

"Man, that bitch had me fucked up! She was just mad because I was dancing with this fine ass nigga, and he didn't want her, so this bitch gon' throw a drink at me and I punched that bitch in her dumb ass face."

"B, you promised me no drunk fights!"

"Yeah, well I lied ok. It ain't my fault bitches hate me but niggas love me."

Shaking my head. I ain't even say nothing after that. I just drove back to Bianca's house.

"So who was that cute ass guy you was dancing with? I seen y'all dance fucking on the floor." Bianca said with a slur.

"Ok, first of all I don't know. Some nigga named Cash. Second, what is dance fucking?"

"When y'all dancing like y'all wanna fuck. Duh."

"Well, we weren't. It was just a harmless little dance. That's it." Although I was curious about what he was really working with.

"Yeah. Ok. Ain't look that way to me. Honestly, seeing you dance with him, I haven't seen you that relaxed in a long time."

"Yeah, well it's over. I'll probably never see him again. I didn't even get his number."

"You didn't get his number?! Aww, Zo what type of shit-blaaaaaah!" Bianca said throwing up in her lap. I pulled over to the side of the road to let her throw up some more, while I cleaned out the passenger side. It was definitely going to smell like throw up in her car for a few days.

When we got back, I helped Bianca up to the apartment and to her bed. By now she was knocked out sleep. I grabbed a blanket from the closet and slept on the couch. For some reason I just couldn't stop thinking about Cash from the club. I could smell his cologne on me and was intoxicated by the scent. And his eyes I feel like I could stare in all day. But who knows, maybe he has a girlfriend on the side or something. You can't be that fine and not have one. Oh well though, only just a memory.

2

CASHMERE "CASH" LOGAN

D riving through the gates to my home, I seen on my clock it was 3 a.m. Parking my 2019 Range Rover in-front, I got out and typed in the code to the front door and entered my 5 bedroom 3 story home out here in Calabasas. I bought this home a while back when I would travel back and forth from Atlanta to here. Originally that's where I'm from and live, but my brother Manny asked me to come out to this event he was having at his club, so I figured why not. It hardly had any furniture in it, only a couch, a 9 piece dining room set, and my king bedroom set. I would have one of my maids come by once a week just to check on it and keep it from getting too dusty.

I went upstairs to the main suite, went inside the bathroom and turned the shower on. While I let the hot water hit my body and face, I started thinking about shorty from the club tonight. Beautiful face, tight ass body, smooth chocolate skin like a Hershey bar. Just visualizing her, made my dick hard. Her pussy was probably so wet too. Next thing I know I looked down and my dick was at full erection with pre-cum coming out. *Damn, I ain't never thought about a chick this hard.*

I turned the shower off, stepped out, and dried off. With the towel wrapped around my waist, I went towards the bed and laid back on it, with the bathroom light being the only light in the room. Drifting off, I imagined shorty on top of me. *I gotta find her.*

The next day, after running around handling some business, I hit up my brother Manny to see if he was good after last night. After that fight that broke out with him and my future girlfriend's homegirl, I kind of left.

"Yoo," he answered.

"Yo what up nigga. What you up to?"

"Shit nothing. Business as usual. What about you? I ain't seen you since last night when you dipped on a nigga."

"Shit, you already know how I'm moving. Ay, what happened anyway with ole girl?"

"Maaaan, I was close to getting to feeling on her pussy, when that bitch Melody walked up talking shit."

"Melody? You mean ya babymother Melody?"

"Nigga who else am I talking about. Anyway, she called shorty out her name and next thing I know I'm watching a female version of Tyson knock Melody out."

"Haha, damn. I told you Melody wasn't no good when you met her. Don't get me wrong I love my niece and all but, nigga that girl is drama."

"Man whatever. You all in my business, who was that piece of chocolate you was dancing with on the dance floor. Looking like y'all wanted to eat each other alive"

"I don't know. I know her name is Zoiena, that's all I know."

"Hmm, doesn't sound familiar, so she can't be a hoe." He laughed.

"Fuck you nigga."

"So damn you ain't get her number?"

"Naw, when ya girl turned into Muhammad Ali, she ran out the club so fast, by the time I got outside she was gone."

"Damn. Yeah I didn't get the other girl contact info either. Maaan, I would've took her home and hammered that pussy." We both laughed.

"But hey, let me call you back though." I hung up and dialed up this nigga name Dex.

"Hello?" He answered.

"Yo Dex, I need a favor. Can you hack the video cameras from my brothers club parking lot?"

"Sure, anything in particular you looking for?"

"See if you can find any footage of two girls running out the club last night. One dark skin and the other brown skin."

"Ight, I got you bro. Give me a little while and I'll call you back."

"Bet." After I hung up, I started driving towards Inglewood to hit up Astro Burger. LA may have been bougie but their hoods had some good food. As I'm driving my phone started ringing again.

"Hello?"

"Hey baby. What you up to?" I looked at the caller ID and seen it was this hoe named Trina. Me and her had been fucking around from time to time. Sometimes she just took that shit overboard thinking we had a whole relationship, and we didn't. She was just some good pussy to fuck on and get a nut.

"What'chu want Trina. I'm out in LA right now."

"Oh." You could hear the disappointment in her voice. "Well I just thought you might want to come by tonight. I cooked us dinner and sent the kids over my mom's house."

"Well, that's not going to happen. Sorry you wasted your time."

"Ok, so when you coming back?" Now she was annoying with all these questions.

"Look, I'll hit you when I'm back. Bye Trina." I hung up the phone. Call me petty, but bitches like Trina needed to know their place. Know when a nigga fucking with you just for the sex or because they really want you. I could never imagine being in a relationship with her, but she had some bomb ass head though that I just kept on lock.

After I left Astro Burger, I made a few more business calls to make sure everything back home was running smooth. I ain't gonna lie, L.A. was beautiful; I loved it out here. Don't get me wrong Atlanta is nice too. But it don't got nothing on these beaches and warm weather.

I owned my own shipping and trading company, also I dabbled in the drug game on the side too, importing cocaine from different countries and selling it to the highest bidder. That's how I made most of my money.

I had two big ass houses, one here and in ATL, and owned my own yacht. I ain't never had to ask a nigga for shit. I grew in a neighborhood where it was either make something of your self and get money or be a stupid ass nigga and die. My brother moved out here a year ago to open up his club, while I stayed. My mom passed when I was just sixteen from suicide and my dad, I haven't talked to that nigga in years. Last time I checked, that nigga wasn't shit to me no way. He was a no good crack addict, who cheated on my mom and made her lose her mind and she shot herself. Shit like that you just don't put your teenage sons through. So I blame that nigga for everything. If it was too hot outside I blamed his ass.

My phone started ringing again, and I seen it was Dex calling me back. Damn this nigga worked fast.

"Yo talk to me." I answered.

"Hey so the two girls that ran out the club last night, got inside a white 2018 BMW coupe. I ran the license plate number and see it belongs to a Bianca Sullivan. She works at the Marigold Café, owned by Zoiena Sulton." This why I loved Dex work. He get down to every detail.

"Ight, thanks Dex; appreciate it." I hung up and googled the Marigold Café. Once I put the address in my navigator I started towards it. I was going to pay miss Zoiena Sulton a visit.

3

ZOIENA SULTON

I had to admit, I had the kitchen smelling so good today. I was making some old fashioned Louisiana gumbo, some buttery dinner rolls, and cheese quiche. Bianca was out today still recovering from her hangover. This was like my second pot today of gumbo because the first one ran out so quickly at lunch time. These L.A. people sure loved them some southern cooking.

"Hey Zoiena, someone's out here to see you." Triston said from the kitchen door.

"Who?"

"I don't know. Some guy."

Looking confused, I washed off my hands, walked to the front and came face to face with the guy from last night.

"Uhh hi."

"Wassup. I was just passing by, thought I get something to eat."

"Oh..ok um...we have gumbo as today's special, with dinner rolls, and cheese quiche."

"Mmm, sounds good. I'll take one order of everything. Along with you accompanying me to dinner tonight."

I laughed at his corny but cute pick up line.

"Thanks, but um...we close at 5, so that wouldn't even leave me with enough time to get ready."

"Ok..well could I at least get your number then. Maybe another time."

I didn't object to his offer. I grabbed a piece of napkin and wrote down my number.

"Here." I gave him the napkin and also went to pack up his food to go. "Triston here will ring you up."

"Thanks. I'll be calling you."

When he left I could smell his cologne lingering. God he was so fine. I would've told him hell yeah I'll go to dinner with him, but I don't know if I was ready to date again. Especially with a man of his caliber. I mean you could just tell he had money from the expensive looking Cuban link around his neck. He could have any girl he wanted, but he wanted to take me out. The thought just gave me butterflies inside, but I decided to play hard to get.

Few hours later, it was almost closing time I washed down the kitchen and started to pack up.

"Zo, can I talk to you for a minute?"

"Yeah, sure wassup."

"Not to get all in your business or anything, but who was that guy?"

"Oh, just some guy I met at the club. Nothing serious."

"Sure seemed like it was serious enough for him to obviously look you up and come to your job."

"I'm pretty sure it was just a coincidence."

"Coincidence?! Zo most niggas take girls home, fuck em, and Uber them home the next morning. Not stalk them, come to their place of business, and ask them on a date."

"Ok, what difference does it make Triston. I told him no anyway."

"Yeah, but you still gave him ya number. Now this clown is going to think he has a chance."

Triston was starting to annoy me now. I never seen him get this upset over me talking to a guy before.

"Chill Triston. Like I said, it's not that serious. Maybe I'll go out with him and maybe I won't. Right now I'm focused on trying to close so we can go. You should do the same."

He stood silent for a minute with this hurt look on his face.

"I actually....gotta get ready to go. I gotta go check on grannie. I already counted today's profits and filled out the deposit form. See you later Zo." He threw his backpack on and left out. Sometimes I really didn't understand Triston. I mean, I didn't get angry when he talked to women that were obviously hoes and sluts. But oh well; he'll get over it.

After everything was shut down for the night, I locked up and went around back to my car. As I'm digging my keys out my purse, I look up and see Cash standing at my car.

"Don't tell me you're going to stalk me now."

"Naw. Not unless you want me to."

"I thought you left hours ago."

"I did. But then I thought I would come back and tell you how good as fuck this food is you made me."

"Well thank you. Is that all you came back for?"

"Naw, I also came back to tell you I don't take no for a answer. I would like if you join me for dinner tonight." His lips were so sexy. I was so distracted with my thoughts wondering how good he would eat my pussy, I almost didn't hear what he said.

"Umm....I mean it's really late. And short notice." I said to try and stall.

"It's only 5:30 sweetheart. And you could just say *no I can't go, I got a man at home and he would be very angry if I went out.*" He said in a fake high pitched voice.

"Well I could say that but I don't have a man at home. Excuse me." I tried moving around him to get in my car, but he blocked me.

"You know I do carry mace." I said but with a smile.

"But you wouldn't mace me would you?" He smiled and I swear the fact that he had dimples made my girl down below so moist. He knew exactly what he was doing.

"If I say yes to dinner, then will you let me get in my car and go home?"

"9:00 tonight. And don't stand me up because you know I know where to find you." He moved from in front of me and went to get in this all white Range. I got in my car and started home.

Once I got home to my one bedroom apartment, I contemplated about not going, but then I kind of made a promise to myself that I would at least give living my life a try. It wasn't that I didn't find Cash attractive. I mean, I was really wishing he would've asked me if he could bend me over in the back of his car. It's just I was afraid to get myself involved with a man again, and he leave me or hurt me. So this date would be just for fun. Nothing more.

Before I got out my car, I noticed it was a bunch of bags in the back that wasn't there before. I grabbed one of them and seen it was a Chanel shopping bag with a note attached to it.

Bought these in advance just in case you would say yes. Which I knew you would anyway. Hope you like, see you tonight.

-Cash

I immediately started blushing. My phone started buzzing and I seen it was a text from a unknown number.

Unknown number: *hope you like the gifts. See you at 9.*

Me: *how did you get in my car?*

Unknown number:*I have ways babygirl.*

I wonder what he meant by that. I hope I wasn't dealing with a psychopath. I got all the rest of the bags out the back of the car and took them upstairs. There was stuff from Gucci, Louis Vuitton, Moschino, and shoes from Balenciaga. Half of this stuff I couldn't even afford to buy on a year's salary. Overall, all this stuff had to be worth over $100,000. After I showered, I tried on this red scrappy dress Cash bought me from Versace. I tied my long dark brown hair up in a bun, and wore the shoes he also bought me. Once I was just about ready, I got a text from Cash.

Cash: *look outside.*

I went to my window and seen that Cash had sent a black Hummer limo to pick me up. I grabbed my Black Birkin bag, that he also bought me, and went outside to the limo. The driver helped me climb in the back, where there was a bouquet of flowers waiting for me and another note.

Roses are red,
Violets are blue,
I'm not no poetic ass nigga,
But I like you.

I laughed at the poem, as I took a sip of the champagne that was in the back. I swear I never smiled this hard on the first date with anyone before, but something about Cash was giving me all the right feelings.

4

TRISTON LESTER

Finally making it home to my grandmother house, I seen she was already asleep. Yes, I still lived with my grandmother but for good reasons. My grandmother was 78 years old and suffered from various health problems, so I felt like if I left her something bad would happen. So after I graduated I decided to stay behind and help her out. Besides she put my name in her will to have the house after she passes on anyway.

OPENING the door to the basement where I mostly stayed, I walked down the creaky steps and turned on the light. All around my room was pictures of Zoiena. Some from high school, some we took together, some I took on the sneak tip. I had articles that the paper had written about her and the café with good reviews, and I even had one that I got blown up to a huge size to cover the ceiling. I had another room upstairs I actually slept in, but down here was like my own personal shrine to Zoiena that no one, not even my grannie, knew about. Plus, I always kept the door locked.

.   .   .

TRUTH IS, I always loved Zoiena; she's beautiful, smart, funny, and everything I could ever want in a woman. I never told her or tried to pursue her because I was scared that she would reject me. Growing up I never handled rejection well; my mom rejected me, my high school basketball team rejected me to play my sophomore year, and if my dream girl rejected me, it would ruin me. Call me crazy but I was determined to make Zoiena mine. I just didn't know how yet. When I saw how she lit up today when that guy walked in asking her on a date, I haven't seen her like that in a long time since her last dude broke her heart, and now this nigga comes along and, from the looks of it, he's about to ruin any chance I have with Zoiena.

YEAH, I'm upset that she's out with him tonight, but our time will come. I'm sure of it. I walk over to this small cubby in the wall where there was all kinds of candles. I lit each one, and pinned up a new picture of Zoiena I took the other day on my phone, and got it printed out at Rite Aid. See, back in the day, my grandmother used to practice voodoo when she was married to my grandfather whose whole side is creole. I must of picked up on a few things, because here I was doing a love spell ritual every other night to get Zoiena to like me. Tonight, I'm going to put a little extra zest into it because I know she's out with that guy. It's not that I was jealous or anything, but homeboy did look good. I'm pretty sure he had every woman ready to take their panties off for him, and that's what I'm worried he will do to Zo. I said a little chant, meditated, and sat in silence for a moment visualizing how I wanted things to go. After all that, I took my clothes off and got comfortable on the sofa bed I had down there.

I FIGURE I would stay down here tonight and watch the flame for the night. Feeling sleepy, I laid my head back closing my eyes, while I imagined Zo laying next to me.

5

ZOIENA SULTON

I had arrived to this restaurant call *Avaloni's,* a Italian spot in Beverly Hills. The driver helped me out, and I walked inside; it was dimly lit, with nice music playing, but there was something odd. Where was all the people? There was only staff.

"Good evening, Ms. Sulton. Right this way." The waiter led me to a booth, where I already seen Cash standing there waiting.

"Thank you, Travis. I'll take it from here." Cash said to the waiter. He nodded and walked off.

I slid in the booth, and Cash slid in across from me.

"So glad you could make it." Cash said to me.

"I am too, but where is everybody? I never seen this restaurant this empty."

"Let's just say I put in a favor to my friend that own this restaurant."

"You just full of surprises aren't you?"

"Sweetheart, you have no idea." He said licking his lips, making me feel wet down there again.

"So what's your real government name; it can't just be Cash?" I asked as the waiter poured us some red wine.

"Why you need to know all that?"

"Because I don't know, you could be a serial killer or something."

"Well, I'm definitely not, but you must be one of those girls that google niggas' names to see what pops up."

"Hey, now days you gotta do that shit, cause y'all be telling half the truth about shit." I laughed.

He gulped his wine down and just smiled. I was just hypnotized at how good he was looking tonight. He had on a navy Tom Ford suit jacket with matching pants, a white button down, hair freshly cut, and his gold Cuban link and shining Rolex.

"So you like me huh?" I asked referring to the note.

"Maybe. Depends on how you act the rest of the night." He said in a sexy tone.

"But why me? You could have any girl you probably want."

"Listen, real men know what they want, and what they like. And right now I definitely like what I see." I blushed so hard that time, I could feel my cheeks touching my ears.

"Logan."

"Huh?"

"Cashmere Logan. That's my full name." He said smiling, exposing the dimple in his cheeks.

The waiter came back with two plates of their shrimp Alfredo linguine and a bottle of wine on ice.

"You know you don't sound like you from L.A."

"I'm not. I'm from Atlanta. Bankhead to be exact."

"So what you doing all the way out here?" I said scooping up my pasta with my fork.

"I sometimes come out here on business. But my brother was having an event at his club, so I made an appearance."

"You mean the guy that Bianca was dancing with? That's your brother?"

"Yeah my baby brother Manny. I'm the oldest and cutest though." He boasted.

I smiled on the inside. Wait until Bianca finds out she was dancing with the club owner.

"So what inspired you to be a chef?" He asked me.

"Well, my dad, he was a chef. He traveled around the world and cooked for a lot of people, so growing up he taught some things here and there. Plus I took up culinary in high school."

"Cool. He must be proud."

"Yeah...he died last year though from cancer." My smile suddenly turned to a small frown.

"Sorry to here that. But don't be sad about it. I'm not no spiritual person or nothing, but he looking down on you. He see how great of job you doing. My mom actually died when I was 16." He said, now playing with his food with his fork.

"Damn. I'm sorry you had to go through that at a young age."

"It's cool. I grew from it, learned from it, and moved on. You can't let your past hold you back from living." He said staring deep into my eyes. It's almost as if he could read me, like he knew what I been through.

We talked a little bit more over dinner, getting to know each other. After we ate, we headed back to the limo and left the restaurant. 20 minutes later we pulled up to this giant mini mansion up on a hill. I'm guessing this was his house.

"Hope you don't mind, I just need to grab something real quick. You can come inside if you want." He said.

"Umm...that's ok. I'll just wait out here."

"Ok. I'll be back." He got out and went inside the house.

About 30 minutes went by, and he still hasn't come back yet. Getting inpatient I got out the limo and walked up to the house seeing the door was cracked open. Stepping inside taking in how huge the place was, and the fact you could fit the whole Beverly center in here, I noticed there was hardly any furniture, but that's probably because he's hardly ever here.

"Hello? Cash you know it's rude to just have your date sitting and waiting for you," I yelled.

I heard some noise upstairs, so I went up the winding staircase, and went inside this huge bedroom that looked like the main bedroom. I heard water running in the bathroom, and started to get annoyed. Who takes a shower in the middle of a date? I banged on the bathroom like I was LAPD doing a drug raid.

"Cash! What's the big idea having me wait in the car for a half hour, just so you could take a shower!"

I suddenly heard the water turning off, and the bathroom door open with him stepping out with nothing but a towel wrapped around his waist. It seemed like the juices between my legs increased more and more, and I found myself unable to hardly talk again from staring him down.

"See something you like? I can tell by the way the drool is coming out the side of your mouth." He said smirking.

I quickly wiped the side of my mouth and switched my face to a more serious look.

"Umm...I would like to go please. It's getting late and I have to open the café tomorrow." I said trying to stay focused.

"Ok. Can I put some clothes on first?"

"Why couldn't you just shower after you dropped me off?"

"Because I knew you would come in and look for me."

I started to get annoyed. "Look, I don't know what kind of games you playing but I'm tired. I have to get up early, and I am demanding you take me home."

"Playing games?" He asked in a low calm tone. He slowly walked towards me, body glistening from drops of water still on him. He was completely covered in tattoos. I wasn't sure if he even had any room. He towered over me with his chest almost touching my chin. Even with my heels on he was still taller than me.

"Real mean don't play games. Like I told you before I know what I like...and right now I like what I see." He said putting a piece of hair over my ear. My body suddenly got the shivers and by now my panties was completely soaked. Thankfully I didn't wear lace.

"I can look in your face and tell you been through some shit ma. Hell so have I. But I also know there's room for healing." He took my hands into his. "If you let me, I can be that healing. But you don't want me to, just say the word."

"I....I..I'm sorry. I can't." I said taking my hands away from his, and walking out the room. I had a few tears streaming down my face, because I wanted so bad to be loved again. I had only knew Cashmere for 24 hours, and already he made me feel like real love did actually exist. But was I ready to risk my heart possibly getting broke for some random guy?

I headed to the front door and when I got outside, the limo was gone. Somehow I think he planned this whole thing out. Feeling stupid for leaving him standing there, I turn to go back upstairs but I seen the light was on in the kitchen. I go to the kitchen and see Cash already dressed in some basketball shorts, and a wife beater, pouring himself a glass of water. He was quiet and didn't even acknowledge I was standing there.

"The limo's gone." Was all I could say.

"His shift is over for tonight. If you need to get home that bad, I can pay for you to get a Uber." He said in a nonchalant tone.

"Umm..no that's ok. I'll just text Bianca to come get me."

"Cool." He said drinking his water.

Starting to feel awkward I decided to say something.

"Cash....listen. You're a great guy, and I will admit I am feeling you. A lot. But I'm just overprotective of my heart right now. After losing my dad, about 2 months after that my ex-boyfriend just up and left town. I haven't been in a relationship since then because I'm afraid. There, I said it. I'm afraid to love again." I said starting to tear up again.

"Listen, I understand what you been through. But damn you not even giving a nigga a chance. I'm not like these suck ass men out here playing around with girls' feelings and shit. At the end of the day I'm a grown ass man, not no boy."

"How would we even begin to be in a relationship? You live all the way in Atlanta and I'm over here. Everyone know long distance relationships don't work."

"That's bullshit. If you want something to work, it'll work. I can fly back and forth and we see each other. That's no big thing."

I started rubbing my temples with my fingers. "This is impossible."

He put down his glass and walked over to me.

"So let's do the impossible then." He said looking me dead in my eyes. After Derrick had left me, I said I was done with relationships, but being here with Cashmere tonight has me feeling a whole different way.

Without saying anything, he took my hand and led me back upstairs to the bedroom. It was dark with only the light from the window shining. He turned towards me caressing my cheek, and his lips met mine. My wetness got to flowing again, making my pussy feel warm and moist. As he hungrily kissed me, like a lost lover, he started to unzip my dress until it was fully off exposing my breasts.

Once I was in nothing but my black thong, he stepped back a little bit and just stood there looking at me.

"What?" I asked. It had been a while since I had been seen naked by another man.

"Nothing. I just....never seen a woman so beautiful before." Damnit. Why did he know what to say at the right time?

He came back towards me and kissed me on my lips, working his way down to the crook of my neck giving me goosebumps all over. Moving his hands all over my body, he removes my panties and makes them fall down around my ankles. Good thing I had shaved, because then he started rubbing on my clit nice and slow.

"Mmm." I moaned feeling all my wetness coming out on his hand.

"Make it wet for me." He whispered with his lips still connected to mine.

He dipped two fingers inside of me going in and out, making squishy noises with my pussy.

"Tell me you want me. Because you been knew you wanted me Zoiena." He said.

"Yes...I..... I want you." I said starting to feel my knees give out.

He started sliding his basketball shorts down until he was completely out of them. I could see his dick was at full erection because he didn't have underwear on underneath. Taking his fingers out my hole, he walks over to the dresser and takes a condom out the drawer. I wanted to ask what he kept those here for but I didn't want to ruin the moment. He put the condom on and walked back over to me; picking me up and putting my legs around his waist, he laid me gently on the bed on my back with him on top. Wasting no time, he put the tip of his head in, and finally I could say I never had a dick this big.

"Oh my god." I squealed. He held himself up with the palm of his hands still sliding the tip in and out.

"Ohhh fuck, Zoiena. I never felt no pussy like this. You tight as fuck." He groaned, breathing real heavily. I guess from me not being sexually active in over a year, my vagina just got extra tight. I only had sex with two other guys before my ex; a guy I went to the prom with, and a one night stand I had in college.

Cashmere knew exactly how to treat my body. He wasn't all rough like he was just fucking me. He was gentle and extra careful with every move he made, which made it feel more like we was making love. Once he stuck the rest of his dick inside, I could feel myself creaming with no control. He put my legs from around my waist to around his neck making him hit my spot even more. At this point it felt like his dick was damn near in my stomach. His pace increased a little bit more going from nice and slow to him starting to pound up against me.

"Let me see that pussy cream one more time. I love that shit." He said looking down while he slid in and out.

"Oh Cashmere. Make me cum, make me cum some more." I couldn't believe that came out my mouth, but I was starting to tap into my freaky side a little bit.

Once I said what I said, Cash threw all the gentleness out the window, and really starting hammering me. I came out at least maybe like 3 more times, before I finally felt that little leg twitch that men do, letting me know he came.

"Ugggh. Fuck. Shit." He yelled, falling to the side of me.

Once we both caught our breath, we both showered, and I

decided to just have Bianca open up the shop in the morning; but before I fell asleep I made sure to text her Cash's brother number and leave the rest up to her. I climbed in bed and Cash climbed in behind me, wrapping his arms around me. I exhaled what felt like a sigh of relief. I pray to God that he was the one.

6
_____

BIANCA SULLIVAN

I wake up the next morning with a text from Zo saying she was "running late" and needed me to open up the café. She thought I ain't know what that actually meant though. She told me about her little boo thang tracking her down asking her out on a date yesterday. So automatically I knew she had to be over his house and spent the night. Ole miss "I got a stick up my ass" finally got some dick after dealing with that punk ass ex-boyfriend of hers.

I AIN'T mad at her though; at least she made sure to send me his brother's phone number. I can't believe the whole time I was dancing on the club owner; I must have looked like a drunk fool in front of him. So before I got out of bed I decided to text the number.

Me: Hey this Bianca. The girl from the other night. I just wanted to say I'm sorry about causing all that trouble the other night, but homegirl had me fucked up. Anyway what's your name so I can store it? text me sometime ;)

. . .

Immediately I got a response back.

Him: Lol, it's all good babe. That bitch was tweakin anyway. You think we can talk about it over dinner at my house tonight? P.S. you can call me Manny. My real name is Emmanuel, but I prefer Manny.

Me:ok, dinner it is. See you tonight.

Getting out of bed, I went to shower feeling super excited about tonight. Manny was fine as hell, and I wanted him to know that he definitely had the green light. Most people, like Triston, would call me a hoe, but I didn't care. I felt like if it's your body, then do what you want with it; just don't be too reckless.

Once I was ready, I left out and made my way to the café. It was already after 8, so I was expecting to see a line outside on this particular day, but when I got there I only saw Triston. I parked my car and got out to go open the door. There was something off about Triston today; I just couldn't put my finger on it. Instead of him saying something insulting to me like he usually does, he look like he was worried about something.

"Bianca, have you talked to Zoiena? It's past opening time and she's never been late before." He said in a frantic tone.

"Well, she texted me this morning and said she was running late, so I'm opening up shop today." His face got more and more worried with each word I just said.

.   .   .

"SHE'S NEVER LATE. So something must've happened. Come on, we going to her house right now." He said starting to walk away.

"WHOA, WHOA! SLOW DOWN." I said grabbing his arm. "I'm sure she's fine, Trist. She went out with that fine nigga last night, so I'm sure he might be the reason she's running late."

HIS FACE WENT from worried to straight angry. In the back of my mind, Triston didn't know I was already aware that he had a crush on Zoiena. Shit, I figured that out when I used to sit in the back of him in our high school math class, and see him write her name all over his notebook. I just never said anything because Triston needs to speak up for himself. If he likes her that much; but I guess he missed out now. Stella got her groove back.

"What if that nigga did something to her? He could've hurt her or worse tried to rape her, and you just acting nonchalant about it."

"LIKE I SAID, she's fine. I'm pretty sure if something happened she would've text us a 911 text or something. Now stop your worrying and let's open up the café. Zo gonna be upset she see us standing here arguing like this." I said making it the end of the convo.

WE OPENED the café and not even 15 minutes later people was coming in. People loved our food, especially my grandmother home made recipes. One day I planned on opening up my own bakery, and everybody from all over will come try my baked goods. Zoiena never treated me like an employee, but more of a business partner. That's what I loved about her. Two hours later, Zo come walking in wearing this huge smile on her face.

"Mmmhmm. Somebody got them some magic stick last night. Finally bitch." I said gloating.

. . .

"BIANCA HOW WOULD YOU KNOW?" She said putting her stuff down and her hair up in a bun.

"BECAUSE DON'T nobody walk around smiling like that unless they got them some. Unless you're just a weirdo."

"WELL THAT'S between me and him."

"OHHH. Oh, that's fucked up. You not even going to tell your best friend about how good the dick was or nothing?"

"NOPE." She motioned her fingers across her lips to pretend like she zippered them shut.

"FINE. Then I'm not telling you my little secret."

"WHAT SECRET BIANCA?" She said mixing some cheese, butter, and herbs in a bowl.

"NOPE. I'm not telling you. I'm not telling you that I got a date tonight at sexy ass Manny's house."

"UMM, ok for one, that's not a secret. I knew sooner or later you two would hook up after I gave you his number. And two, sounds like it's going to be more going on than y'all two eating food."

.   .   .

WE BOTH LAUGHED. I hope I didn't come off too hoe-ish to Manny, but I knew what I wanted when I wanted it. In the middle of us enjoying butterflies from our new found flings, Triston walks to the back and grabs a bottle of water out the fridge.

"Hey Trist." Zoiena said cheerfully.

"HEY." He said in a dry tone and walked back to the front.

WE BOTH LOOKED at each other. " Uhh, what's with him?" Zoiena asked.

"I DON'T KNOW. Maybe it's that time of the month."

"What time of the month?"

"OH GUYS HAVE time of the months too. You know when they get moody, horny, and act like grown babies all at the same time. The only difference is they don't bleed like us."

WE BROKE OUT LAUGHING. I was confident that Triston was just jealous that Zo is dating again, being that he did have a crush on her. Even still, I never seen him this mad before.

"HE'LL BE FINE. He's probably just mad that he the only one not getting any."

She shrugged it off and continued preparing the special for today.

FINALLY IT WAS CLOSING TIME, and I was exhausted. I had a 100 cupcake order, somebody came in wanting my famous pineapple upside down henna cake, and everyone came in ordering berry tarts for some reason. Even though I was tired, I still had a little bit of energy left to go home, shower and get dressed to go over Manny's house. I wore this extra short ruffle skirt, my v-neck crop top to show off my cute pierced belly button, and combed my long straight hair up into a bun. I grabbed my Louie bag and was on my way.

THE ADDRESS MANNY gave me was 40 minutes away all the way near Ventura. I understand they got nice houses but damn why this nigga gotta live so far? I arrived to this huge ass mansion and pressed the buzzer for the gates to open. Once they did, I drove up the long as hell driveway and parked my car. I stepped out, seeing Manny was already there at the door waiting; and I didn't know whether to laugh or cuss him out. Here I was all dolled up and he got on sweatpants with a white t-shirt looking like he just got out of jail.

"WELCOME TO ME CASA SEXY." He greeted me.

"THANKS FOR THE INVITE, but uhh...why you dressed like you just didn't feel like getting dressed?" I said walking into the house.

"WELL I DIDN'T, but I figured you wouldn't like me if I smelled like sweat from me working out earlier so I decided to shower."

I JUST LOOKED at him with one of those "are you serious" looks, but then got distracted by something in the air smelling good.

"MMM, something smells good. What's for dinner?"

· · ·

"Everything pretty much. Shrimp, steak, lobster, duck; you name it my chef can cook it for you."

I could get used to this.

This place was like a castle. He had a huge chandelier in the foyer, with cathedral ceilings, and expensive looking art everywhere. He showed me the indoor 10 seat movie theater, basketball court, and huge swimming pool. It had to be at least maybe 7 or 8 bedrooms in here.

We sat down at the huge dining room set he had that look like it was made for a medieval court.

"Can I get you anything to drink madame?" Asked this guy in a penguin suit.

"Uhh, I'll just take some Chardonnay."

"Chardonnay? Pshh, that's child's play. Ben bring out some Dom Perignon. It's some in the basement."

"Right away sir." He hurriedly walked away.

I looked at him in astonishment.

"Wow. You have your own waiter."

"Yeah. I don't really like going out to restaurants, so I hired my own personal chef and waiter. Plus I pay them better then any fancy pants restaurant would."

.　.　.

"Impressive." I said already getting turned on by his sexy ass smile.

Ben quickly came back with a bottle and two wine glasses. He poured us our drinks and informed us dinner will be out shortly. Five minutes later he bought out some lobster tail soaked in butter, mashed potatoes, steak, and a plate of soft ass dinner rolls. If it was one thing I loved it was good ass dick and good ass food.

"So tell me more about yourself Miss Bianca." He said eating a piece of steak. "Other than the fact that you fine as fuck."

"Well, I'm 25, graduated college with a business degree, went to culinary school after that, and I just work at the bakery with my Zo. I like to eat junk and watch Netflix on my days off, party and have a good time."

"Shit, I could see you was having a good time the other night the way you was twerking all on a nigga."

I blushed a little from embarrassment and some from being aroused. Sometimes when I drank, I can be a whole new creature.

"But that's dope that you know how to bake though. Most females only know how to do hair and make-up, or want to be a model. That's different, I like that."

"Thanks. So what about you?"

· · ·

"WELL, I'm a man of different trades. I opened up my nightclub a year ago. I also own few gym franchises, and part owner of the *Zıo* nutrition drink company."

I NODDED STUFFING a big piece of lobster in my mouth, and slipped on some of my wine I never had before. It was bitter tasting, but was still good. I looked over at Manny just staring at me.

"WHY ARE YOU STARING AT ME?"

"OH, so I invite you in my house, cook you dinner, bring out my good wine, and I can't stare and admire how beautiful you actually are?"

"TECHNICALLY, your chef cooked this. So no. Try again."

"YOU KNOW I see you got a smart ass mouth. Don't worry though. I got something for that." He said licking his juicy lips.

MY PUSSY INSTANTLY GOT WET. I sipped some more of my wine to keep myself from blushing even more.

"So who was that girl at the club? The one I had seeing stars probably the next morning."

"UGGGH. I KNEW THAT WAS COMING." He said rubbing his hands over his face. "Ok, so one other thing you should know about me is I have a daughter named Destiny. She's 4 years old and that was her mom Melody clocking my every move as usual."

. . .

WHEN HE SAID that I almost choked on my food a little bit. Why the hell is he just now telling me this?

"SOOO, when was you going to mention that to me?"

"I WAS AT SOME POINT. But I just wanted to see how far we could get first. I usually don't like telling women I got a kid when I first meet them."

"WHY? Are you ashamed of her or something?"

"NO OF COURSE NOT. I love my little princess, but most women when they hear there's a kid in the picture, I never hear from them again."

"OH." I said in a low tone.

"THAT'S why I am the way I am. Get pussy, and count money." He said throwing back the rest of his wine.

I NUDGED him in his arm.

"I HOPE you don't use that same philosophy with me."

"WELL THAT DEPENDS ON YOU." He said biting his bottom lip. "So we'll see."

.   .   .

FOR THE NEXT hour and a half, we talked and got to know each other while occasionally hinting sexual remarks towards each other. Ben eventually brought us out a fruit platter with melon, grapes, and strawberries. After a while that wine was starting to really take over.

"So what's your plans for the future?" I asked sitting on the table in front of him.

"MMMM, I don't know. Maybe open up another nightclub somewhere. I'm thinking Miami or Vegas. And maybe becoming like a sponsor for athletes." He said now caressing my thigh.

"WHAT ABOUT BEING IN A RELATIONSHIP? Like being married and stuff?"

"I DON'T KNOW. I don't really think about stuff like that. So many women out here you know."

I don't know why when he said that I got instantly jealous. But the Gemini in me got off the table and sat in his lap, with the front of me facing him.

"LET ME TELL YOU SOMETHING, you tell them other bitches, that I'm in the picture now."

"OH IS THAT SO?" He said as I could feel his dick hardening.

"YUP. YOU GOT A PROBLEM WITH THAT?"

"NAW...NOT AT ALL." He whispered in a low tone.

. . .

WE BOTH LEANED in and kissed like our lips was made of magnets. His hands went under my skirt and started squeezing my ass. I started taking off my shirt, showing my DD-cup breasts.

"DAMN." He said taking my nipple into his mouth like a newborn baby.

"MMM, UGH THAT FEELS SO GOOD." I moaned.

I TOOK OFF HIS SHIRT, exposing his six-pack and smooth brown skin. He then started untying his sweatpants and ripped them down to his ankles, along with his Versace boxers. We stopped kissing for a minute because I had to pause. Now I've seen a lot of dicks before, but Manny's dick had to be the biggest I've seen. I was little scared to put it inside me; but my pussy was saying otherwise. The way I was leaking wet right now, my pussy was saying "bitch take that dick. Take one for the team."

"DON'T BE SCARED; he won't hurt you. Much."

"NIGGA PLEASE, I AM NOT SCARED." I lied through my teeth.

HE WALKED over to the wall and dimmed the lights on the chandelier that hung over the dining room table.

"WAIT WHAT IF YOU STAFF SEES?"

. . .

"THEY WENT HOME for the night. So we good." He said picking me up and sitting me on the table.

We started kissing again, as I felt the tip rubbing up again my clit. My cum was already coming out. He eased his way in sliding in and out.

"OHHH FUCK!" I screamed.

I leaned back on my back and he climbed on top of me. Holding my leg up with one hand he began pumping faster and faster making me cum with each stroke.

"FUCK BIANCA, your pussy good as shit." He groaned. "Ain't no way I'm letting this pussy go."

I don't know if it was the wine, but I liked the sound of that.

"FUCK ME, Manny. Fuck me like I need to be." I squealed.

Suddenly, he flipped me over from my back to my stomach. Before he could get started, I decided it was time to take control. I arched my back putting my butt in the air, like a dog in heat. Once he stuck it back in, I started throwing it back, making my ass cheeks clap against his skin.

"Damn, baby. You know how to take the dick." He said holding onto the sides of my hips.

He slapped my ass a few times, and I could feel myself about to cum again.

"Oh Manny, uhhh...Ohh." I came all over his dick. I think I even squirted.

Once Manny was about to cum, he pulled out and let it go in his hand. Making me realize we didn't even use a condom. Once I got in my right sober mind I was going to bring that up.

. . .

WE CLEANED ourselves off in the kitchen and headed upstairs for round two. Man, what a night.

7

ZOIENA SULTON

These past two months have been nothing but pure bliss. Me and Cash have been going out exclusively, and the intimacy was always on 100% every time we saw each other. Every week he would fly over to L.A., we would spend most of the time together when I wasn't working, and he would go back. That was always the saddest part. I planned on flying to Atlanta to spend the weekend with him soon and see what things was like out there. During this time, I just felt so open with him; and I haven't felt this way in a long time.

TODAY WAS SUNDAY, and the café was closed, so me and Cash decided to go sailing. Although I wasn't a sea person, I would try to make it work. We arrived to Marina Del Rey by 10, and the weather was nice and breezy as usual.

"Hey don't get all motion sick and throw up on me. This outfit was expensive." He joked.

"BOY, nobody is going to get motion sick."

.   .   .

"Yeah, don't say that now, then be leaned over the rail looking green."
He laughed.

"Shut up."

I wore a Moschino bathing suit, with some jean shorts, some Gucci
flip flops, and my sun hat. Of course Cash only wore some swim
trunks and a grey wife beater, with some Nike slides. For him to only
be 26, he wasn't like all these young flashy niggas wearing designer all
the time. We got to the boat and met a man with grey and black hair.
    "Zoiena, this is Philip. He's going to be driving the boat today."

"Hello."

"Nice to meet you. Everything's all set up. If you need anything at all
please don't hesitate to call me."
    We nodded and stepped on the boat. I never been on a boat this
nice. There was a downstairs area that had a one bedroom with a
mini bar and bathroom, a area for sun bathing, a kitchen, and small
eating area for dinner later. We went downstairs first as the boat
started to take off from the marina.

"This is so nice. It's been a long time since I been on the boat." I said.

"Damn, don't tell me a nigga took you on a boat before I did."

.   .   .

"No, crazy. My dad used to take me sailing when I was little. His best friend owned a boat, so he would take me fishing and everything."

"You really miss ya dad huh?" He said sitting on the edge of the bed.

"Of course. But I'm sure he would be happy that I'm living out my dream and continuing his legacy."

"True." He paused for a minute and just stared at me. "Come here."

"I walked over to him and sat on his lap."

"You know I'm captain on this ship right?" He said kissing my arm.

"Wait..you own this boat?"

"I own a lot of shit. I also own this too." He said putting his hand between my thigh.

"Stop nasty."

"What? It's mine. Come on, let me get a quickie right fast."

"No Cash. Later. After dinner I promise."

.   .   .

"Fine. But you owe me some extra good head too."

"Done."
We shared a kiss and went up top.

The rest of the day we spent having fun and enjoying each other's company. We took a few cute photos for social media, but I didn't really post anything too much anymore. Until now.

"Look." Cash showed me his phone. Manny had sent a picture of him and Bianca at the beach laid up together. I swore they was always in competition with us about who was having the best date.

Later that evening, I changed out my bathing suit and into a cute mini dress by Chanel. We planned having a candlelit dinner tonight to end things off. I had to admit I was feeling a little down because Cash was flying back tomorrow. A part of me wondered and hoped he didn't have another woman or something back home, but I wanted to trust him.

I met Cash on the top deck where they had set up a nice table with two chairs, a candle in the middle and bread. Real romantic like. Cash had changed into some Robin jeans and a Dolce and Gabbana button down.

"Mmm, we might skip dinner and just have you for dessert you keep wearing that around me. Getting me all excited and shit."

"OMG, sit down."

.   .   .

WE SAT at the table and tried some of the bread. Within ten minutes, Philip brought out some plates of fried clams, soup, and a bottle of Hennessy on ice.

"So Miss Sulton, what are your plans for the future? Other than being my future wife."

I SMILED at that last comment. "Well, I want to one day open up my own cooking school. So that people can know how to cook food that feed the soul and mind."

"OK. And also having my baby right?" We both laughed.

"MAYBE. I'LL THINK ABOUT IT."

"YOU BETTER NOT HAVE NO other nigga baby. If you do I'll fuck that nigga up and chop his motherfuckin dick off." He said licking his lips.

"CASH, CAN I ASK YOU SOMETHING?"

"SHOOT." He said with a mouth full of clams.

"WHAT WAS your relationship with your mom like?"
He looked down at his plate, with this sad look on his face.

"IT WAS OK I GUESS. Some of the time she was actually my mom, and the rest of the time she was worried about my dad. What he was doing, who he was with...that type of shit."

. . .

"OH. HOW ABOUT YOUR DAD?"

"...I don't talk to him much but I know the nigga. Let's just say our relationship ain't the best. That nigga could die for all I care."

"WHY DO you feel that way? He's your dad. You only get one."

"WHAT ARE YOU A THERAPIST NOW?"

"No, I'm just saying, whatever differences you two have, can you put it to the side and build a relationship."

"No. Fuck that nigga. He ain't shit but a deadbeat who put my mother through hell." He said looking like his eyes was getting watery, but he was holding it back.

"LISTEN, Cash-."

"No, you listen Zo. I don't wanna hear shit else about this nigga. He's dead to me. Far as I'm concerned I don't have no father. So drop the shit." He said real upset.

I got quiet because that was the first he ever got mad at me. Whatever his dad did must have been terrible, but I'm sure he would tell me sooner or later.

"Look, I'll be downstairs." He said getting up from the table and taking the whole bottle and Hennessy with him.

. . .

I JUST SAT THERE WONDERING what I said wrong. My dad was the one person who meant a lot in my life and treated me like a princess;but now he's gone. Life is too short to hold grudges against people, no matter how bad they did you wrong. Once you leave this earth none of that shit is going to matter anyway.

After sitting there for five more minutes, I got up and went down below. I found Cash sitting on the edge of the bed throwing the liquor back straight from the bottle. Not saying a word, I walked over to the radio and turned it on low.

I feel, lately when I get up in it you be actin different
You feel, putting your feelings all in it gon be detrimental...

I was surprised we could get a signal out here. "Like you love me" by August Alaina was playing and it set the prefect mood. I unzipped my Chanel dress and let it fall to the floor. In nothing but my Vickie Secret lace thong, I walked over to Cash who now had put the Henny down, and was completely focused on me. I stood in front of him, while he moved his hands up and down my legs, and kissed my stomach.

I GOT down on my knees and started unbuckling his pants. Once his dick was out, I took it into my mouth.

"Ohh shit." He moaned.

I swirled my tongue around, while bobbing my head up and down his shaft. I let it go back all the way to my throat, and surprisingly, this time I didn't gag. When I first started giving him head, I would choke because it was too long and thick. I stroked his balls with my free hand, making all kinds of slurping noises with my mouth.

"FUCK ZO. You already makin a nigga cum, and I ain't even ya pussy yet."

Soon as he said that I went all in. I moved my head faster and would occasionally come off to slobber on it, making it more wetter.

"Shit. Baby, I'm boutah cum." He said grabbing the back of my head.

I let him release in my mouth and swallowed like a pro. He lifted me up, and laid me on my stomach with my ass up. He stroked his dick to get it back hard, and once it was, he rammed it inside so fast, I had to cover my mouth to keep from screaming.

"Who told you to suck my dick that good?" He said panting, while he held me down with his hands.

"Oh my god Cash. Cash, don't do my pussy so hard like that." I moaned in a high pitched voice.

"This my pussy. I can do whatever I want." He kept pounding me, making me strain from having a orgasm back to back.

"Cash...Cashmere....I love you." I accidentally let slip out. We only knew each other for a short time, but already I was telling this man I loved him. Maybe it was the dick, maybe it was something else; it was something about this man that had me feeling right. I just hope he felt the same about me.

"*Girl, if you just fuck me like you love me*
    Fuck me like you love me,
    Fuck me like you love me..."

. . .

HE GROANED extra loud letting me know he came.

"Fuck. Phew. Girl that pussy is deadly." He said grabbing a nearby towel and wiping himself off.

A HOUR and another round later, we arrived back to the marina. We went straight to his house, showered, and went to sleep.

THE NEXT MORNING, I was running late to the shop, again, which was normal when I spent the night over Cashmere's house. I got up, got dressed and made my way to the café. Bianca texted me letting me know she was going to be late too. I guess her and Manny had a long night too. I get to the café, and jet to the door, but to my surprise it was already open. Maybe Bianca got here earlier than she thought she would.

I WALK to the back and see Triston instead. Lately, he's been real stand-offish; not replying to none of my texts, not hardly speaking to me, or acknowledging me.

"Hey." I spoke first.

"WASSUP." He said still looking down at the counter he was wiping off.

NOT WANTING this to be like this between us, I decided to speak on it.

"Triston, can we talk for a minute."

HE SHRUGGED. "IT'S YOUR STORE."

"I been feeling lately like there's been some tension between us. And I wanted to know why?"

. . .

HE STOOD quiet for a minute and finally spoke. "Zo, since I known you, you been like the little sister I never had. So out of instinct, I feel like it's my job to protect you. This random ass dude comes along and you're head over heels for him and don't even know shit about him. You and Bianca prance around here all day long, like y'all so in love, but I'm telling you that nigga is no good. I can see it in his eyes he mean you no good."

"BUT YOU'RE WRONG TRISTON. Cash, he's sweet and gentle when it comes to me."

HE RUBBED his hand over his head. I never seen Triston this upset before about me dating before. I get that he felt protective of me, but at the end of the day, I was still grown enough to make my own decisions.

"YOU KNOW WHAT FINE. Do whatever you want. But don't come crying to me when he breaks your heart."

"FINE. Now can we please squash this."

"WE CAN SQUASH IT.....IF you make me some lemon pepper wings later." He smiled.

"DEAL."

. . .

AROUND NOON, it was busy as usual. Bianca and Triston both couldn't decide on who should go on their break first, so they both went leaving me to hold down the store by myself. I swear it seemed like every guy that came up to the counter was trying to get my number. It's always Triston up here running the register, so I hardly ever have contact with the customers.

"HEY THERE PRETTY LADY?"

UGH. *Here we go.*

"HI, HOW CAN I HELP YOU?"

"WELL, I'll take some apple cinnamon bonbons, with a side of your number."

YUCK. I could almost gag at the corny pick up line, and if that wasn't worse, his breath smelled like he ate a whole pack of shit mints.

"UMM SORRY. I'm already seeing someone."

"AWW, come one. Ya man ain't gotta know about us. We can keep it our little secret." He said with a sly smile.

"BUT WHAT IF her man finds out anyway?" Cash said from behind him.

· · ·

THE GUY TURNED AROUND and looked like he was about to shit bricks.

"HEY MAN, I was just-" before he could finish, Cash picked him up by his shirt with both hands.

"WHAT I ADVISE for you to do is get the fuck outta here with ya halitosis ass breath, before you end up being on a fucking feeding tube for the rest of ya life." He put him back down and the guy quickly ran out.

"BABE, you know you can't be scaring off my customers like that." I said impressed with him coming to save me.

"I CAN'T. But I can scare off corn ball ass niggas who try to get at my girl though."

"YOU RIGHT. So what time does your plane leave?"

"IN A FEW HOURS."

"DO YOU HAVE TO GO? Can't you stay for one more day?"

"YOU KNOW I wish I could. But business is calling. Plus, I gotta check on my house."

"WELL, then maybe I just have to move out there then."

.   .   .

"Maybe, But we'll talk about that later. Before I leave, I wanted to give you this."

He pulled out a velvet box with a bow on it. I opened it and it was a rose gold 14k Cartier bracelet with my name engraved in it.

"Aww Cash, thank you, I love it."

"You betta love it, as much as it cost. It was either that or a new PlayStation."

I laughed, I love how much he had a sense of humor.

"Well, let me get to this airport. You know how LAX is. You get there early and still miss your flight."

"Ok. Call me when you land."

He nodded his head and left out the door. I was going to miss him.

8

MELODY PRIEST

"When I see yo ass I'mma fuck you up myself, you bitch ass moutherfucka!!"

THAT WAS like the sixth voicemail I left on Manny's phone. He knew what he was doing. He knew ignoring me would make me angry. Here I was sitting up in the house still recovering from when his little slut he met at the club punched me in the face and broke my nose. I had to have reconstructive surgery and everything. Then he had the nerve to be posted up with the bitch on Instagram. Buying her gifts, taking her out, loving her instead of me.

I STILL FOUND myself loving Manny, no matter how bad he treated me and cheated on me. Before I got pregnant with Naija, me and him was the prefect couple. Once he found out I was having his baby you would've think it continued, but noooo. This nigga had bitches on top of bitches calling his phone, popping up at the house, saying I was lying about being pregnant. He almost believed them bitches until I showed him the sonogram. Now here I was, stuck with a baby and a broke nose. How was I going to find me a new nigga with a nose like Michael Jackson?

"MOMMY, can we go to the park?"

I swear my daughter had to ask the stupidest questions at the wrong time. What the hell I look like going outside with bandages still wrapped around my nose.

"Naija, go sit down and play with your barbies or something."

"BUT I WANT to go to the park and play."

"NAIJA, I said no! You see these bandages on my face?! Your daddy new hoe did this to me. So go sit down and get out of my sight."

SHE WALKED BACK out the door with a sad little look on her face. Yeah, sometimes I treated her mean, but I called it tough love. She was going to learn early that this world don't love you and neither do these niggas."

I FELT MY PHONE BUZZING. Excited I thought it was Manny calling me back. I quickly grabbed it off the night stand but seen it was just my plastic surgeon calling.

"HELLO?"

"HI MS. PRIEST, this is Doctor Kletcher. I was just calling to say today's the day. You can remove the bandages from your nose anytime you like. Just be sure to rub some aloe Vera on it twice a day for scaring."

"OK THANK YOU DOCTOR."

I hung up, feeling a little happy. At least I won't have to walk around looking like a mummy any more. Then I noticed I had a unread text message from Manny. I quickly opened it.

Baby daddy: stop calling my phone you crazy bitch, before I get a restraining order on you.

I THREW the phone on the floor enraged. Who do he think he is, prancing around with a bitch that disrespected and embarrassed his own child mother. Well I'll show him. I got up and walked to the bathroom and started taking the bandages off. Once they was all off, there was some mild scarring but nothing make up couldn't fix. Dr. Kletcher was the truth. He was the best plastic surgeon in L.A. His prices was steep, but when you offer some fire Pussy like I got, the best things come for free. I walked out the bathroom and picked up my phone off the floor. I scrolled through Manny's Instagram to see if I can find this bitch page. And I did: cocogal27. Manny had blocked my original page, so I had to make a fake one just to troll his.

I CLICKED to send her a friend request, but her page was public so I thought I would look through it. She was a nice looking girl, with a bomb ass body. Most of her pictures always consisted of her baking something or some kind of pastry. I'm not going to lie, I was low key jealous but knowing Manny, this, whatever it was, wasn't going to last long. He was going get tired of her and come running back to me and his family. So I'll let him have his fun for now, but sooner or later, he was going to have to get it together and realize we are meant to be.

9

CASHMERE LOGAN

A fter a long five hour flight, I finally made it back to the A. I picked up my Bugatti from the monthly pay parking lot, and peeled out of the airport traffic.

"*All my grizzly niggas sta-stackin again, big old forty on me, back packin again, keep a quarter on me, back pack in the Benz..*" I ain't gonna lie; it felt good to be home, but I was missing my bae. Riding home listening to "Bacc At It" by Yella Beezy, I was wishing I didn't have to fly back and forth, but what she didn't know was I just needed to tie up some loose ends and then I planned on moving to L.A. permanently. I was already talking to a few realtors and architects, about a new house. A house just for me and my shorty. Shit, the way we always fucking, maybe a few mini shorties too.

I MADE it home to my eight bedroom estate, which consisted of a huge swimming pool, basketball court, indoor movie theater, and a separate garage for all 26 of my foreign cars. You may wonder why did I need such a big house and it was only me living here. Well, growing up on the streets I came from nothing. After my mom offed herself, the state wanted to separate us and put us in the foster care system.

But I wasn't letting that happen, I hustled while my little brother went to school, and provided for both of us. Once I got my bread up, I bought my first car. I'll never forget it, a 96 Chevy Impala. Then that's when the hoes started pouring in. Speaking of hoes I ain't heard from Trina all week; maybe she finally got the message.

I PARKED OUTSIDE of my house and keyed in the house code on the lock pad. I opened the door and was shocked to see Trina standing there with nothing But lingerie on. Looks like I spoke to soon.

"Hey baby. How was your trip?"

"TRINA, what the fuck are you doing here? How'd you get in here?"

"DID YOU FORGET SILLY. You gave me the code one night when you wanted me to come over."

I made a mental note to change the locks later.

"HOW'D you even know I'd be here?"

"UMM...MARIA TOLD ME." She said referring to the housekeeper.

I KNEW she was lying because Maria knew better than to tell her my whereabouts without my permission.

"WHATEVER. Don't let the door hit you on the way out." I said walking right past her. I walked all the way upstairs to my master king bedroom, with her right on my heels.

· · ·

I PUT my stuff down and sat on the edge of my bed. Trina stood in the doorway looking like a lost puppy.

"CASH, what's wrong baby? I thought you'd be happy to see me."

"WHY WOULD YOU THINK THAT?" My answer looked like it stabbed her in the chest.

"I…I thought we was in a good place. You told me you loved me."

NOW I KNOW this hoe has to be delusional. I would never tell her no shit like that.

"TRINA, understand me and understand me clearly. I never for the life of me told you no shit like that. I don't know what type of crack you smoking, but you need to go about your business."

SHE STARTED TEARING up like that was supposed to shake me. "Is it somebody else?" She asked lowly.

"WHAT DIFFERENCE DO IT MAKE. What I do and who I do it with is none of your business. Now you either going to show yourself out or I can have Baldwin and Chops show you out." I said talking about my two pet pit bull dogs.

SHE SNIFFLED LETTING the rest of her tears flow down. She walked over to where she laid her clothes, got dressed and ran out the door.

Stupid ass hoe. She need to be worried about who her children's father was, instead of worrying about who I'm fucking with.

TAKING OFF MY CLOTHES, I showered, had my cook make me up some fried chicken and greens, and turned to the ESPN channel on my 65". When I started feeling sleepy, I remembered to text Zoiena goodnight and let her know I made it back.

M*E*: *made it home safe. Thinking of you. Miss you.*

I COULDN'T EVEN WAIT for her to reply back, because a nigga was suffering from jet lag and some more shit. I turned the TV off and drifted off to sleep.

10

TRINA MURDOCK

I sat in my red 2018 Chrysler, trying my best to not have a mental breakdown. I couldn't believe the way Cash was treating me now all of a sudden. When we started dating, he was such a gentleman to me. Now he just treats me like a random slut, without a pot to piss in. I was starting to feel like it was another woman involved in his life that he didn't want me to know about. Tapping into my stalker skills, I opened Instagram on my phone and went to his brother Manny page. I seen he was posted up with a new chick that I had to admit was cute and hair was laid in every picture. I know his babymother wasn't liking this though. I met her when she and Manny flew over here to Atlanta, and she was on him like white on eggshells.

I scrolled through his page to see if I could find anything, and for a while I couldn't. Until I got to this picture from a few weeks ago that had Cash in the background with his arms around some dark skinned girl. Bingo. I knew he wasn't flying back and forth to Los Angeles for nothing. Next thing I did was went on Manny's girl page. They had to know each other or something. I scrolled through her page and found a picture of them together. I clicked on this bitch screen name and seen her page was private. From her profile I learned her name was Zoiena Sulton and she owns a café called *The Marigold*. I don't know why but that last name Sulton sounded familiar. I shrugged it off, sent her a friend request, and started driving towards my friend Janice house.

So this is the bitch making my man forget where home is. Well we'll see about that. I drove across town to Buckhead, and parked my car outside the two story house. Janice lived in a much better neighborhood than I did. That's only because she got pregnant by some big time lawyer; not that I was hating or nothing. Ringing the door bell I could hear footsteps walking to the door.

"Girl, what are you doing over here this time of night?" Janice said snatching the door open.

"Because we need to talk." I said walking inside and prancing over straight to the liquor cabinet. I began pouring some Amsterdam into a cup and threw some back.

"Uhh...are you ok? Where your kids at?" She asked.

"They at my mom's house." I said sitting down on the couch. "And hell no I'm not ok. Cash is fucking around with another woman."

"Well shit I figured that. Any man who don't at least call to see if you breathing, definitely don't give a shit about you."

"Yeah, but the problem is I love him, Janice. Yeah, I know we never made it official, but I know we have a fighting chance."

My phone dinged letting me know I had a notification. It alerted me that Zoiena had accepted my friend request. I instantly started going through her photos, and seen her and Cash have been spending a lot of time together. He buys her gifts, takes her on dates, and a bunch of other shit he's never done for me. It felt like I was going to be sick.

"Trina, maybe this is a sign. There are plenty of other men out there to love on. Cash isn't the only one."

"But he's my only one. Do you know how tiring it is to start over? I would rather keep dealing with Cash and his bullshit, than to start over with a fuck nigga."

"So what are you going to do?"

"Right now I'm going to wait it out and give him his space. You know me, I always got a plan up my sleeve." I said with a grinch smile.

"Giiiirl, why don't you leave that man alone? What's so special about him anyway?"

I guess it was true when they say money will change you. If I can remember, Janice was a gold digging scheming heifer like me. Now that's she's married and all this good shit, she such a saint.

"Janice, who side are you on? You suppose to be down with whatever."

"I am but I'm just saying this is stupid. You're a grown ass woman with four kids, chasing after a man that doesn't want you. Who has time for that."

I heard enough. I got up and walked towards the door.

"Whatever Janice. You have your opinions and I have mine. Watch; I'll show all y'all I'm not the one to fuck with." I left out, getting back inside my car.

Sitting in my car for a little while, I scrolled some more through this Zoiena girls page. She wasn't even all that compared to me, so I didn't understand why Cash was fucking with her. Whatever the reason was didn't matter because once I came up with a plan to break them up, she was going to regret even meeting him.

11

BIANCA SULLIVAN

They do anything for clout, do anything for clout
 Look, whole lotta people need to hear this,
 It's lotta names on my hit list,
Mouth still say what it want to,
Pussy still wet like a big bitch..."

I WAS FEELING good this morning, getting dressed, while shaking my ass to "Clout" by Offset and Cardi B playing on the built-in Bluetooth system. I loved their relationship; it was classy with just the right amount of ghetto and freaky.

"KEEP SHAKING ya ass like that, I'm going to have to bend it over." Manny said from the doorway.

"SO COME BEND IT OVER THEN." I said bending over, putting my hands on my ankles and swaying my ass back and forth.

· · ·

ME AND MANNY relationship been going great these past few months. I spent most of the time at his house and hardly at my own. Just to get clothes and whatever else I needed. Also, to make things better, no pop-ups from baby momma.

"OH, SO YOU TEASING ME HUH?" He said walking over slapping me on the ass.

I stood up and turned to face him. We started tongue kissing and made our way to the bed. I pushed him down on his back and started taking off his pants and underwear. Once I got his dick out, I wasted no time putting it in my mouth. I slobbered on it letting it hit the back of my throat.

"SHIT, Bianca. Fuck, don't go so fast. I don't wanna nut yet."

I went up and down while jacking him off with my hand at the same time. I sucked him off for another five minutes, until he came down my throat.

"MMM, DELICIOUS." I said, taking off my panties and bra. I climbed on top of him and slowly eased myself down on his dick.

"OHHH MY GOD." I moaned throwing my head back.

"*AND IF YOU wit it like I'm wit we can get it crackin,*
    I'm trying to give you two things some dick and satisfaction..."

"LOVE JONES" by YG was playing, and it was setting the mood so right. I started cumming like a water fall as I bounced up and down.

. . .

"Aww fuck ya pussy good as shit. Come on let's cum together," Manny groaned holding on to my love handles.

"Uhhh, uhhh, uhhh shit." I cringed as I came so much, some of it got on the bed, even with me on top.

I got off of him and laid down next to him on his chest. He put his arm around me and it felt so comforting. I was off today, so other than go shopping, I didn't have no plans.

"Hey, you want to go to the carnival today down Long Beach?" I asked. He gave me this unsettling look.

"Actually, I meant to tell you....my daughter is actually supposed to come over for the weekend."

My butterflies instantly turned into nervousness.

"Manny why are you just now telling me this?"

"I just found out this week. See me and Melody went to court months ago over custody of Naija. My daughter is my world and Melody isn't fit to be no mother. She's selfish, self-absorbed, and a hoe on top of that."

"So why did you get her pregnant?"

"I mean, she wasn't always like that, but after she had my babygirl and I seen the way she started treating her, I said fuck that. I want to be in her life at all times. Melody stopped me though because I didn't want to be with her. She went to the courts lying saying I was abusing her and they granted her full custody with no visitation." He said looking sad.

I STARTED FEELING BAD. This whole time I thought he was just low key being a deadbeat father, not even going to see his only daughter, but turns out it was his bitch ass baby momma doing.

"GRATEFULLY I GOT the best lawyer money can buy that got the judge to grant me visitation every weekend, until we go back to court. I just received the papers in the mail this week and I was going to tell you, but didn't know when."

"WELL, I am mad that you didn't tell me, but I didn't have a dad growing up, so I do encourage you to be in her life."

"OK, well I sent my assistant to pick her up, so she should be here in a hour."

"A HOUR?! Oh my gosh I gotta shower, put my face on.." I said hopping up and jetting to the bathroom.

WHILE GETTING MYSELF TOGETHER, I started playing in my head how meeting Manny's daughter for the first time might go. What if she didn't like me? What if she had a smart mouth on her like most little girls? What if she was bad like those kids off *Are we there yet?* I began to wonder all of that until I heard the doorbell ring.

. . .

I WALK DOWNSTAIRS to see Manny opening the door and letting in the cute little girl with pigtails and light up tennis on.

"DADDY! I MISSED YOU," she said hugging him.

"I MISSED YOU TOO PRINCESS." He picked her up and walked over to me. "Naija this is Ms. Bianca., daddy's new friend."

"HI, NICE TO MEET YOU." I said.

"HI, can you do my hair like yours, it's so pretty."
    Hmm, maybe this wasn't a bad idea.

"MAYBE ONE DAY. If your dad lets me."

"OH HE WON'T MIND, he just my dad." We both laughed at her remarks.
    "Well how about this, we can discuss your choice of hairstyles after we go to the carnival." Manny said.

"YAYY, CARNIVAL!" She jumped for joy.
    We all headed out to the car and was on our way to the carnival. Maybe being step mommy wouldn't be so bad. Or at least for today.

12

MANNY LOGAN

I had to admit I was hell of skeptical about being in a relationship with Bianca. When my mother was killed, I never had a stable relationship when it came to women. Just one night stands and situationships mostly, but never a real relationship. The thing I loved most about Bianca is that she knew what she wanted and was determined to go get it, with or without a man. Most of these broads wanted you to take care of them while they lay at home all day, like this was the 1960's. I didn't mind doing that, because I had enough bread to take care of both of us, but I also liked a woman that had her own shit going on. Not to mention her pussy was like crack to me, and I was always feenin'.

WE GOT TO THE CARNIVAL, and had a blast. We got on the Ferris wheel, the merry go round, and got to watch Bianca throw up; I told that girl not to eat all those corn dogs, but she just don't fucking listen. After she cleaned herself up, we went to the petting zoo area.

"OHH, look daddy baby ducklings. Can I have one please?"

. . .

"Now Naija, what are you going to do with a pet duck?" I asked already knowing the answer.

"We gonna have tea parties, and play dress up, and play barbie dolls."

"Sounds more like you need a little sister then." Bianca said looking at me. I liked the thought of having another child, but I preferred a son next time. Someone I can play baseball with and teach how to holla at girls.

Suddenly, I felt something nibbling at the back of my pants. I turn around and see a huge as goat standing behind me.

"Ahh, what the fuck!" I backed away from it and it came closer until it had me cornered.

"Aww daddy the goat likes you."

"Y'all don't just stand there, get this thing before it try to eat me." I said trying to push it away.

"Manny don't tell me you're scared of a little goat." Bianca bust out laughing.

"Oh y'all think this shit funny." I said. I reached over in the feeding bin and grabbed a ear of corn and threw it so it would follow it, and gratefully it did.

Bianca and Naija started laughing so hard that tears was coming out. Even though I was mad they was laughing at me, I felt good seeing them getting along so well. Which made me love her even more.

AFTER WE LEFT THE CARNIVAL, Naija was knocked out sleep. I carried her to one of the guest rooms, and had Malia, my on call nanny I hired, to wash her up. Bianca went upstairs to take a bath, while I sat in the living room to watch the game. Ten minutes into the game, my buzzer ringed letting me know someone was outside. I looked on my phone connected to my outside camera, and seen it was Melody. I was stunned because Naija wasn't supposed to go back home until Sunday, so what fuck was she doing here.

I GET up and walk to the door opening it.

"You better have a good reason for being here." I said pissed off that she was at my door.

"I DO ACTUALLY. I came to see my daughter and kiss her goodnight."

"WHAT? No Melody. This is my weekend. You've had her most of the time and now it's my turn."

"I HAD her most of the time, yes. But who fault is that Manny."

"UHHH...YOURS. You know I wanted to be in her life. You're the one who went to the court and lied because you're a bitter ass bitch. Little do you know you fucking up right now, because you breaking our agreement with the court."

"WELL I NEVER MADE AN AGREEMENT FOR my daughter to be over here, with you or that slut ass hoe you with."

I SIGHED as I just shook my head. "Yo what do you want from me? Money, child support? What?"

BEFORE I COULD REACT, she jumped on me, wrapped her hands around my neck, and kissed me. I quickly pushed her ass off me.
    "Yo what the fuck are you doing?"

"MANNY, don't act like you don't still want me. Look, you need to wrap up whatever you got going on with that bitch and come back and be with your family."

"ARE YOU FUCKING INSANE? You come to my house, unannounced, and try to kiss with my girl upstairs? Like, do you wanna die?"

"MANNY, I know I been a pain in the ass lately, But it's only my way of yearning for your love, and wanting us to be a family again. I promise I'll be submissive, I'll fuck you every night like a wife should. Just tell me what I have to do and I'll do it."

I LOOKED at her long and hard. "You know what you can do for me right now? Get the fuck off my doorstep." I slammed the door in her face, and walked away.

. . .

"Babe, who was that?" Bianca asked from the top of the steps.

"Nobody, just someone trying to sell something."

"Oh ok. You coming to bed?"

"Only if you promise to give me some nasty sloppy head first." I said smiling.

"Ok, I promise." She said slowly walking to the bedroom.

Melody has lost her goddamn mind if she think I was going from this good ass life right here, to her bullshit and her drama. Honestly, other than my daughter, Bianca was the best thing that's happened to me in a long time.

13

ZOIENA SULTON

It's been almost a week since I last seen Cash, and I was missing him BAD. I would wake up in the morning thinking he was there, but it would just be my pillow. We FaceTimed almost every few hours, and half the time I couldn't even focus at work because I missed his sweet voice. He said he had to handle some business, so that's why he couldn't fly in this weekend, but he promised the next time he came he would stay for a whole week.

Tonight I was going to an event with Bianca at Manny's club; there was this new rapper by the name of Real Bagz that was having a record deal party and everyone was pulling up. Of course Bianca was just going to meet me there after having one of her many fuck sessions with Manny. Speaking of sex, ever since me and Cash started having sex more and more, it was like I craved it. Tonight I was wearing an all-white strapless Gucci dress, with some black red bottoms, and my MCM purse.

As I'm styling my hair into curls, I hear a knock at the door. I wasn't expecting anybody, so to my surprise it was Triston at the door. He had on a True Religion Jean Jacket, with a black and blue striped shirt, some black jeans from express, and all black Jordan air sneakers.

"Triston? Hey, what are you doing here?"

"Well, I thought we could go to the party together. After all I am your best friend." He said.

"Umm, I thought you didn't like going to clubs?"

"I typically don't, but hey, what the hell. You only live once."

"Ok, well let me just do my make up and I'll be ready." I had a sudden weird vibe, and wondered why Triston all of a sudden wanted to go out. I ignored my thoughts and finished getting ready.

After beating my face, we was out the door and on our way to the club. The line was literally wrapped around the building. Lucky for us I had passes so we went straight inside.

We slide through your block wit them stickz

We Aimin at you wit a dick

Thirty clip let it hit

These bullets hit you like a ritz......

The club was super packed with everyone dancing to "Coca Cola" by TNT Tez. I spotted Bianca and Manny over in the VIP section, already drinking and dirty dancing on each other. Security checked us and let us through.

"You two gon' end up having a baby, keep dancing on each other like that." I said.

"Bitch finally, I thought you wasn't going to come." She said giving me a hug. "I see you brought out the stick in the mud." She looked Triston.

"I see your wig is still intact." He fired back.

"Whatever. Manny, this is my other mentally incapacitated friend from high school Triston." Him and Manny dapped each other up.

"Manny, have you talked to Cash. He's not answering his phone," I said, not having talked to Cash since this afternoon.

"Naw I haven't heard from him. But I'm sure he'll "pop" up". He said looking at me strangely. Is it me or is everyone acting abnormal tonight.

I brushed it off and took one of the shots on the table.

After a hour went by, I was feeling good, while me and Bianca was dancing on each other in the VIP section. It seemed like every guy and female was trying to get in and party with us, but couldn't.

"Hey, you mind if I cut in." Triston said in my ear.

"Of course." I said in a tipsy tone. Me and Triston went out on the dance floor, full of people.

Girl you workin wit some ass, yeah, you bad, yeah

Make a nigga wanna spend his cash, yeah, his last yeah...

When Juvenile "Back That Ass Up" started playing, I lost all control. This was my jam back in high school; if this came on you better knew what you was doing.

"Ohhhh shit, this my jam." I said as I started dancing on Triston, and like the anti social person he was, he just mostly stood there. I was so into it, I didn't even notice him feeling on my butt. I quickly stood up, turned around and just looked at him, and he stared at me like he didn't know what to say.

"Y'all having fun?" Said a familiar voice from behind me. I turn around and I see Cash, looking like the sexy Greek god he is.

"Cash, this is just Triston. He's my friend from high school. You seen him before; he works at the shop....we was just dancing, I swear..."

"You don't gotta explain. Bianca already told me." He said not even looking at me, but straight at Triston. "You the cashier right?" He said kind of sarcastically.

"Yeah, But Zo's my homegirl. I love her like a sister." Triston replied back nervous like.

"I see. Well your homegirl is my girl now, ya dig. And I don't mind y'all hanging out and all, but you keep your hands to yourself." He said real sternly, creating a awkward silence between Triston and him.

"Come on Zo. We leaving." Cash said grabbing my arm.

"What? Wait! I just got here; the party just getting started."

"Don't let me say it again. Now you either gonna walk outta here voluntarily, or I'm going to carry you out of here on my shoulder. You pick."

I pouted like a little kid and stomped my way to the exit.

Although I was excited to see him, I don't appreciate him popping up, talking to my friend like that, then making me leave the club. I would call and apologize to Triston in the morning, but right now I needed to deal with this.

I got in the passenger seat to his Benz wagon, and we drove off headed towards his house.

"Who gave you the right to tell me what to do? And why you didn't tell me you was coming back?" I said upset.

"First of all, I earned the right when I put my dick inside that tight ass pussy of yours. Second, I decided to pop up on ya ass, and I'm glad I did."

"Yeah, but you didn't have to talk to my friend like that, Cash."

"Talk to him how? All I said was keep ya hands off my girl. How is that wrong?"

"Ugh. It wasn't what you said, it was how you said it."

"Man fuck all that. That nigga knew what he was doing. I know you saying that's your friend and all, but something ain't right bout him."

"What? Oh, come on."

"I'm serious. You know I can read people and spot bullshit from a mile away. I can look in this nigga eyes and tell something off. Like a light switch."

"Listen, Triston has been my friend for years. I'm sure if there was something wrong, he would tell me."

"Yeah, ok. If I was you, I would keep my distance."

"Whatever." I said ignoring him. Now he was really tripping.

We pulled into a nearby gas station, because his tank was almost on E.

"Wait right here, Ms. Twerk team." He said jokingly. I shot him the middle finger.

He got out to pump the gas, while I sat in the car. I texted Bianca letting her know that Mr. Bigstuff is in his feelings and we left already. I kept hearing Cashmere's phone ding back to back, and was curious to know what it was. I unlocked his phone, and saw it was text messages from a girl named Trina.

Trina: I had fun the other night
Trina:when you coming back home
Trina:me and the kids miss you

That last one really made my stomach turn. The other night? Kids? I couldn't believe my eyes. This whole time Cash had been living a double life. That's why his ass ain't want to move to Los Angeles, so I wouldn't expose his ass. My head started hurting as I tried to hold back my tears, but my vision started getting blurry from water in my eyes.

Cash returned to the car and I didn't say a word. We left the gas station, and as soon as we made it to his house, I quickly hopped out the car, and started walking down the driveway to leave his house.

"Zo? Zoiena! Zoiena!"

I could hear him calling me, but my mind was blacked out. I immediately started calling a uber to come pick me up. Cash ran to catch up with me, and blocked my path.

"Move Cash!"

"No, not until you tell me why the fuck you acting like a psycho."

"Why don't you ask your fucking girlfriend back home and your kids, why I am."

"What the fuck are you talking about? I don't have no kids."

"Oh right. So I guess the bitch Trina was lying then."

"What? Wait, hold up, you was going through my phone?"

"It doesn't matter! You obviously been lying and been cheating on me this whole entire time, and I can't believe I actually trusted you!"

"Check this shit out. Never have I fucking lied to you. Like I told you before I'm not no fuck ass nigga. I'm going to be honest, me and Trina did use to fuck around but before I met you. All the fuck she trying to do is get to you and you letting her." He said while standing real close to my face.

"Maybe I am. I'm so tired of you niggas thinking you can just get away with shit like this, and we supposed to be dumb and just go along with it!" I said with tears streaming down my face.

"Zo, I'm going to tell ya ass this once. Get the fuck inside and let's talk about this." He said clenching his teeth together.

"No I'm not doing shit! Why don't you go hop back on the plane and go be with Trina!." I said turning back around to continue to walk away.

Cash come up behind me and picks me up, throwing me over his shoulder. I started kicking and screaming, and beating him in the back.

"Put me down! Put me down Cash!." I screamed.

We finally get up to the house, and he carried me inside finally putting me down.

"You are fuckin impossible Cash. How can you get mad at me about having a innocent dance with Triston, but you living foul?"

"Yo Zo, watch ya mouth ight." He said getting closer to me, with his cologne invading my nose. Damn, why'd he have to smell so good.

"And what if I don't?" I said not backing down.

We stood there for what seemed like 5 long minutes, until he grabbed the back of my neck and roughly kissed me. I wanted to resist, but I couldn't. My pussy started to feel moist, and I returned the affection putting my arms around his neck. He picked me up putting my legs around his waist, and carrying me all the way upstairs. We got to the bed and started undressing each other, while still kissing. He lifted up my dress, and began feeling on my clit.

"Ohhh." I moaned.

He pulled his dick out from his boxers, and rammed it in. Stroking me while putting my legs around his neck, and grunting really loud.

"I told you I wasn't letting you go. I told you that shit. You cant leave me, Zo. I need you." Cash said.

I was speechless from the way he was hitting my spot, making me cry from total bliss. Yes, I was still mad at him about those text messages, but the part of me that loved him wanted to believe he wouldn't hurt me.

"When you told me you loved me, I wanted to say it back so bad. But I was afraid. But I'm not anymore. I know this is where I want to be. I love you Zoiena." He said kissing my neck.

"Ohh Cash." I squealed as he started speeding up making me cream all over his dick. "I love you too Cashmere." I said back.

We both climaxed together and waited a moment to catch our breaths. Once we cleaned ourselves up, we both climbed in the bed together.

"Cash."

"Yes babygirl." He said with his arms around me.

"Promise me. Promise me you'll never hurt me."

He looked at my with the light from the window shining on his face.

"Zo, I can promise you that. And so much more." He kissed me on my forehead as we both fell asleep.

You can say I was putting my heart at risk with Cash, but isn't that what you do when you really love someone? You take all the risks.

14

MELODY PRIEST

Manny had me fucked up if he think I was not going to fight for my family back. The fact that he had my daughter over his house with him and his new bitch, made me enraged. He thought he was slick posting pictures of them at the carnival, but at the end of the day I was Naija's mother whether wanted to be or not.

TONIGHT MANNY WAS HAVING a event at his club, and I was pretty sure him and his hoe was going to be there. I got there and convinced the bouncer to let me straight in. Even though Manny had me on the do not enter list, flashing a little titties can go a long way. Once I got inside the crowded club, I ignored the few niggas that tried to talk to me, and spotted Manny over in his usual section. Of course him and his pocket pussy was there, looking like they didn't have a care in the world. I got me a drink from the bar and stood there until it was time to make my move.

AFTER ABOUT A HALF HOUR, Bianca finally left out the section and headed to the bathroom, and that's when I made my way over. I showed security my boobs, and got straight in. When Manny seen me he instantly frowned; seeing as though he had about 10 shots, and was obviously drunk as fuck, it wouldn't take long for my plan to work.

"OH, hell no, Melody! What the fuck are you doing here? You know you not allowed in here." He said drowning another shot.

"OH COME ON. Is that any way to treat the mother of your child."

"WHEN SHE BEEN ACTING like a total nut, yes. It is."
    I walked over to him and set my drink in the table.

"LOOK, I just came here to say, I'm sorry. About everything. About dragging you to court, keeping Naija away from you, showing up at your house. Everything."
    He looked at me, this time with a forgiving facial expression.

"LISTEN, you my child mother. Only thing I need you to do is take care of her. That's it." He said.
    "Ok, well would you at least do me the pleasure of dancing with me." I said stepping in front of him and grinding on him.
    I was wearing a cute but tight, purple long sleeve back out dress I found onFashion Nova. They might have had some cheap prices, but they're stuff was dope.

SURPRISINGLY MANNY DOESN'T RESIST, and start letting his hands roam all over my body. I started grinding my ass on his dick, feeling him get hard.

"Oh look my new work like to work out
She in the mirror tryna workout, like workout
L-l-Look, look, look, look
Pole dancer, pole dancer, pole...."

THE DJ STARTED PLAYING one of my new favorite songs "Pole Dancer" By Wale, and it had me feeling untouchable. I decided it was time for step 2 in my plan, and turned around to start making out with Manny. He actually accepted, and returned the kiss by putting his tongue down my throat. After we finished, I noticed out the side of my eye Bianca was standing there looking lost.

"BIANCA...I.." Manny said, But was caught off guard when she threw a drink at us, and ran off.

My hair got a little wet, but I was so delighted that my plan worked I didn't even care. Manny ran after her, and almost fell over trying to chase her. I fell out laughing at his stupid ass.

MISSION ACCOMPLISHED.

15

CASHMERE LOGAN

After fixing things with Zoiena, I hopped on a red eye flight the next morning to Atlanta. Getting off the plane, I picked up my car and headed straight to my destination. I parked my car outside of Trina house, walked up to her door, and started banging on that shit like I was the police. She came to the door in a little tight ass shirt, and booty shorts.

"CASH, what the hell you knocking so hard on the door for early in the morning? You going to wake my kids up."

Without saying anything, I grabbed her ass up by her neck and pushed her inside. I hemmed her ass up against the wall, with her trying to fight me off, but of course I was too strong.

"LET me tell ya hoe ass something, if you ever text my motherfucking phone again, or so much as accidentally call me, I will break ya fucking jaw." I said clenching my jaw. "You know I'm not one for putting my hands on females, but bitch you tried me one too many times. Stay in ya lane and know when a nigga doesn't fucking want you anymore." I said releasing her and letting her fall to the floor. She started choking and gasping, but I didn't care. This slut was going to learn today, you don't come for me or mine. I left out her little funky ass townhouse, and hopped back in my car on my way to the crib.

MAKING it to my estate only thing was on a nigga mind was taking a hot shower, laying down for a minute, and facetiming my shorty later. I park my car, and get out to see Maria my housekeeper at the front door.

"OH MR. LOGAN, you have a visitor in the living room waiting for you. I tried telling him you weren't here, but he insisted on staying until you got back."

WONDERING who the hell she could be talking about, I power walk to the grand living room to see who was invading my home, and might gotta get their shit split open. I turn the corner to see it was my father.

"SON, long time no see. I see you doing real well for yourself. This is a beautiful home you got here; you could house a whole football team in here."

"WHAT DO YOU WANT OLD MAN?" I said not up for the small talk.

"WHAT, can't an old man come say hi to his son."

"NOT WHEN HE'S been gone for most of his life."

. . .

"...Look I know I messed up with you, your mother, and your brother, but that's why I'm here. To make things up. It's never too late."

"what?! Nigga you damn near pushing 60 and you wait until now to try and work things out? If it's money you after you can forget it."

"Son I don't need your money. I know what I use to do back in the day far as the drugs and women. But I'm clean now, I started this program, and it's been really helping me. I even started reading my bible and going to church again."

"My nigga I don't care if Jesus himself came down here and put the crown of thorns on your head. The fact of the matter is you abandoned the only woman that was down for you, and your two sons. And now you want to come by my house unannounced, and try to kumbaya with a nigga. Fuck outta here."

"Cash, I know you think I'm to blame about what happened to your mom-."

"You are! When you left, she didn't know how to deal with raising two boys on her own and no help, so she lost her fuckin mind and killed herself. All because of you."

"You can't blame me for that! We was young, I didn't know shit about raising two kids."

. . .

"OH RIGHT, so the best thing to do was go somewhere else and lay up with another bitch."

"YOU CAN'T BLAME me because your mother wasn't strong enough to handle a little bit of pressure."

I stood there for a minute with my nose flaring, then I stormed off to my office where I handle most of my work. I went in my desk drawer and grabbed my 9mm semi, went back and pointed at his ass. He put his hands up, looking like he was going to piss himself.

"WHAT I ADVISE you to do, is stay far the fuck away from me before I blow your fuckin brains out. Get the fuck out!"

He picked up his briefcase and ran out the front door. The nerve of this nigga coming in my house telling me what my mother went through. Seeing all of that at a young age was traumatic enough, and he wants to try and make up for years later. Fuck him! I swear it was too many people trying me lately, first Trina, then Zoiena's bitch ass friend, now my father.

I PUT MY GUN AWAY, and went upstairs to shower and FaceTime Zoiena. Her smile was the only thing that could make a nigga feel better right now.

"Hey baby." She said looking like she was still at the café.

"HEY WASSUP."

"NOTHING JUST EATING lunch in my office. You ok; you look mad."

"I'M STRAIGHT. I had a run-in with my father today."

. . .

"How'd it go?"

"Do you gotta ask, you should've known how that shit went. I told him go fuck himself and to get out."

"Uggh, Babe listen, I know you hate your father-"

"No hate is too light to use in this situation. I despise that nigga."

"I know, but...don't you think it's time to let the past go and at least try and see if y'all can work things out."

"Yeah, when hell freezes over."

"Cash, I'm serious. If I learned one thing from going through what I went through it's forgiveness. Yeah, my parents ended up not being together, but I still dealt with it the best way I could."

"You know speaking of your parents, how come you never talk about your mom? Is she dead too?"

"No." She said looking off to the side. "She lives in Riverside. With her new husband."

. . .

"OHHH, and I get it you don't like him or something?"

"No."

"WHY NOT? Your Momma gotta have a life too."

"I KNOW BUT....I just felt like she moved on way too fast. Like how do you get remarried three months after my father just died."

"SOMETIMES, people have to cope in their own ways Zo."

"YEAH, well every time I went over there he was always trying to bond with me like I was his daughter. So I stopped going." When she said that I couldn't help but bust out laughing.

"WHAT SO FUNNY?" She said.

"I'M SORRY BABE, you mean to tell me that you stopped fucking with ya mom and stepdad all because he was trying to build a relationship with you?"

"YES..NO.... I DON'T KNOW."

"LISTEN BABYGIRL, I tell you what...if you can patch things up with ya mom, then I'll "think" about maybe talking to my dad. Deal?"

. . .

"...OK DEAL."

"SO ENOUGH ABOUT THAT. When is you coming to out here to the A, to see me?"

"WHEN YOU DON'T HAVE thirsty ass hoes chasing after you."

"I TOOK CARE OF THAT. This hoe know wassup."

"YEAH NOW THEY PROBABLY DO."

"THAT STILL DON'T ANSWER my question though."

"THIS WEEKEND. I'm taking some personal time off and leaving Bianca in charge, so I can fly out there then."

"IGHT, cool. Make sure you show up with nothing but a coat and some heels on too." I said licking my lips.

"OMG, BYE." She said hanging up.

I ain't going to lie; I was super excited that my baby was coming to see me. Shit, I might tie her ass up so she don't got to go back to LA.

16

BIANCA SULLIVAN

This had to be the worst week of my life. Manny's lying cheating ass fucked around with the wrong bitch. I was outside the Bcom Fitness gym that he owned, and I knew he was going to be there. Without bringing any attention to myself, I snuck to the parking lot, and found his lime green Lamborghini he loved so much. I looked around for any cameras or people sitting in parked cars. When I seen the coast was clear, I took out my favorite jumbo butcher knife and jammed it hard into the back tires. Once I was done, I hurried up and ran back to my car and sped off.

ALL WEEK I had been sitting in the house, not going to work and perfecting my craft all because of what happened at the club the other night. Usually I wasn't the type to cry over no nigga. I would just block their number and move on to the next one, but Manny held a different place in my heart. For the first time I was actually in love with someone, who accepted me for me. All that got flushed down the toilet when I caught him tonguing down his babymother at the club, when he was supposed to be there with me. After that he called and texted my phone non-stop and kept trying to apologize. I wasn't buying it; drunk or not, it should've been no reason you had your lips on her.

I GOT BACK HOME to shower and get dressed. It was 8:00 in the morning, and I was in charge of opening up the shop this weekend while Zoiena went on her little rendezvous with her man. I noticed I had a text message from Manny and a missed call.

Asshole:I'm sorry Bianca. I've said it a hundred times. But my Lamborghini though?

Me: *Fuck you.*

I threw my phone on the bed and went to handle my hygiene.

WHEN I ARRIVED to the shop, I didn't see Triston standing out front waiting for me. Come to think of it I haven't seen Triston or heard from him since the party, when Cash ran him out the club. He thought I didn't see him running out the club crying. Part of me kind of felt bad for him.

I TRIED CALLING HIM, but got no answer. I decided he would probably show up; he was just running late. I opened the café, and rushed to get everything ready. By lunch time, I still didn't see or hear from Triston, which was very unlike him. I felt like a slave rushing back and forth between the kitchen and cash register. The phone was ringing off the hook, the line was almost out the door, and I burnt my strawberry crème cupcakes. I called Zoiena phone, but I got no answer. So,I figured she was on the plane and couldn't answer the phone.

ONCE IT WAS CLOSING time it took longer to clean up and shut down than it would have when all three of us is there. Wondering what happened with Triston, I called him again and still got no answer. I started getting a bad feeling. I knew where he lived, but never been to his house. I put the address in my phone, and got in my car to head there.

WHEN I GOT to the address in Watts, I parked my car at the corner and walked to the one level house. I knocked on the door, and an elderly woman with long grey hair answered the door.

"Umm, hello ma'am. I'm a friend of Triston. I was just wondering if he was here. I can't seem to get a hold of him."

"OH, ARE YOU HIS GIRLFRIEND?" She asked and almost made me gag.

"UH, NO WE'RE JUST-."

"WELL COME ON IN! Welcome to the family!" She said inviting me in.
I just went along with it and went inside.

"TRISTON ISN'T HERE RIGHT NOW, but he should be back later. You're more than welcome to wait. I'll be in my room though. I was watching the lottery; grandma need her a billion dollars."
I laughed at her as she walked to the back.

I WENT in the living room and seen she had pictures of Triston from the time he was a baby to when he graduated high school. Triston never talked about his family to us much, except that his mom just one day left him over his grandmother house, and hasn't been back since.

·   ·   ·

I THEN NOTICED A CRACKED open door that looked like it went to the basement. I looked to make sure his grandmother wasn't coming, and opened the door. I tiptoed down the creaky steps and seen a glowing light. When I got to the bottom of the steps, I couldn't believe my eyes.

There was pictures of Zoiena everywhere! The walls was covered, and even the ceiling. I felt like I was in a bad horror movie and I was the person who discovered the killer. Never would I have thought Triston was this fucking crazy. I knew he might've liked Zo a little bit, but not on no obsessed type shit. This was beyond insane; this was straight up psychopath.

I walked over to a little cubby where there was candles with Zoiena craved in it, pieces of paper with *Zoiena and Triston* on it, and a bunch of oils. Getting freaked out, I decided to leave, and hopefully warn Zoiena about this. As I was getting ready to leave, I heard voices upstairs and footsteps coming from the back of the house. I quickly looked around for a place to hide, and found an old coat closet in the wall. I got inside and remained real quiet, as I heard footsteps coming down the stairs. I peeked out the door a little bit and seen it was Triston. Scared to death, I started peeing on myself a little bit. He pulled out a black candle from his pocket, and lit it with a match.

"Ancestors old and wise, be with me here tonight. Break them up as soon as you can. Show Zoiena that I want to be her man." He inhaled and exhaled, sat there for a minute, and blew out all the candles until it was pitch dark. He started back up stairs and I was at ease that he didn't see me.

WHEN I WAS sure it was safe, I turned on the light from my phone, and tried to find another way out. I seen there was a basement window, but it was really small. If I was 50 pounds smaller, I probably could've fit. I was going to have to try, because there was no way I was spending the night down here in the devil's basement. I walked over to the window and pulled myself up to open it. Once I got it open, I put my head and arms through first; but when it was time for my hips to go through I got stuck. Now was the time to wish I didn't fill out at a young age. I sucked everything in and pulled and tugged to get unstuck. After 5 minutes of pulling and tugging, I finally got unstuck and went completely through the window. I found that the window lead to the backyard.

"Oh, Triston your back." I heard Triston's grandmother talking to him from a open window. "A pretty girl came by here, and was looking for you."

Oh no.

"What girl grandma?"

"I don't know her name. But she was brown-skin with pretty eyes, and long black hair." Once Triston realized she was talking about me, he rushed out the front door. I went out the backyard down the alley, and when I made it to my car, I hurried up and got inside. I sped off and headed back home. I called Zoiena but still got no answer. I was getting a incoming call from Triston; I ignored it but he called again. I sped up and made it to my apartment. I drove into the gated parking garage, and got out the car,,while Triston is blowing my phone up.

"Bianca." A voice said from behind me startling me, but when I turned around it was Manny.

"Don't do that! You trying to give me a heart attack now."

"Uhh...sorry. You ok, you seem shaken up." He said.

. . .

"I'M FINE MANNY, now what do you want?"

"I WAS JUST COMING to apologize. I was drunk, but that doesn't justify
anything."

"WELL I DON'T ACCEPT, so excuse me." I said trying to get past him,
but he blocked my way.

"MOVE OUT MY WAY MANNY." I said getting frustrated. He walked back
to his car, and got something out the back seat. He returned with a
brown box.

"WHAT'S THIS?" I asked.

"JUST OPEN IT." He said handing it to.

I TOOK the lid off the box, and seen it was a German chocolate cake,
with a bride and groom figurine, and the words *"I'm sorry. Take me
back."* Damnit. He knows German chocolate is my favorite. I looked at
him this time with a calmer expression on my face.

"BIANCA when I'm with you, I feel like God blessed me with my other
half. And I don't want something like me being a stupid man, make
you go to the next man." He pulled out a red velvet box that had a
gold David Yurman bracelet in it. "Please, let's start over."

·   ·   ·

I PUT the cake box on the ground and put my hands around his neck for a hug. Just when I got the chance I slapped the hell out of him.

"Oww! WHAT WAS THAT FOR?" He asked.

"IF YOU EVER DO THAT shit again, you better start planning out your funeral." I said.

SUDDENLY HIS PHONE STARTED RINGING. He dug it out his pocket, while still rubbing his face.

"Hello?.....Yes....What?!.....is she ok?!...ok I'm on my way." He hung up and started running back to the car.

"WAIT, MANNY WHAT HAPPENED?!"

"IT'S NAIJA. She's in the hospital!"

17

MANNY LOGAN

I had to be doing about 70 mph on the highway, with my foot never leaving the gas pedal. At this point I was ready to go off; my daughter was my entire world, so if anything happened to her I would be lost in this world.When me and Bianca got to the hospital, we rushed inside to the nursing desk.

"Excuse me, I'm here to see Naija Logan. She's my daughter." I said to the secretary.

"Ok, have a seat over there, and the doctor will be out in a minute." she said while still talking on the phone.

"But is she ok?" I asked her, but she ignored me.

See what I didn't have time for, is ignorant ass bitches.Especially, when my kid was involved. I snatched that phone out her hand and threw that shit.

"Ok sir, you need to calm down and have a seat, before I call security."

"Bitch, fuck you! I'm trying to ask you about my fuckin daughter, and you being a rude asshole." I yelled getting irritated.

"Manny, come on; let's just go sit down and wait." Bianca said. If it wasn't for her being here to calm me down, this hospital would've got burnt down.

We went over to the waiting area and sat down. I put my hands on my head, trying to calm my nerves and keep from turning up in here. After two hours went by, I was a nervous wreck. Bianca came back from the cafeteria with two cups of coffee.

"Here. Thought you could use this." She said. I took the cup, but didn't even have the energy to drink it.

"The parents of Naija Logan?" This white, bald guy came out and yelled.

"Me.... I'm her father." We both stood up.

"Hi, I'm Dr. Daniels. So your daughter suffered a fracture to the arm. She just got out of surgery. She'll be fine. She's asleep for right now from the anesthesia, but you can go in and see her now."

"Thank you doc." I said.

We both rushed in the back to her room down this long hallway. This weekend was my weekend that Naija was over my house. I had left her with the nanny, while I went to Bianca's to try and apologize to her. I couldn't wrap my brain around how she could've fallen and broke her arm, but I sure as hell was going to find out when I got home.

We got to her room, where she was knocked out sleep. I went over to her and rubbed her head. They had a purple cast wrapped around her arm, from her wrist to her upper arm. It pained me seeing my shorty like this.

"Oh my god, what did you do to my baby?" Melody said from the doorway. "And what is she doing here?" As if things couldn't get any worse.

"Melody, not now ok."

"No, you're lucky I don't call the cops on ya ass. My baby broke her arm while you out here chasing hoes." She yelled.

"Who you calling a hoe?" Bianca said getting closer to her.

"Hey, hold up." I said coming between the two of them. "You two not going to do this around my daughter."

"For all we know she could've broken her arm." Melody said going over to Naija and acting like she was so concerned.

"Trick, you lucky we in this hospital right now, but keep on talking ya shit. I'll break ya nose again."

"See. This is the type of shit you have around my daughter Manny."

"Melody, stop acting like you so concerned. Only reason you had Naija was because you thought you was getting a check." I said exposing her truth.

"Fuck you Manny!" She screamed.

"Hey excuse me, but you're going to have to lower your voices or I'm going to have to ask y'all to leave." A nurse came in and said and left back out.

"Look Melody, why don't you go back home. I'll call you when she gets discharged."

"I'm not going anywhere." She said crossing her arms. This girl was impossible.

There was a knock at the door, and it was white lady with short blonde hair dressed in a suit.

"Yes, can I help you?" I asked.

"Hi, my name is Karen Anderson. I'm with Child Protective Services." My heart suddenly sunk to my stomach.

"Ok, what do you want?" I asked getting defensive.

"Well, I actually need to speak with the parents. Privately." She said looking at Melody thinking she wasn't the mom.

"Whatchu looking at me for? I'm her mother; that bitch ain't nobody." Melody yelled.

"Bitch, keep talking shit, and you going be in the hospital next." Bianca fired back.

"B, can you just give us a minute." I asked her. She left out the room and went back to the waiting area.

"So how can I help you Ms. Anderson? What's this about?" I asked.

"Well, Mr. Logan, when paramedics found your daughter, she was at your residence alone. There was no one else in the home with her, and she had fallen down the steps."

I wore this confused expression on my face, because that didn't sound right. When I left Malia was there giving her a bath.

"Mr. Logan have you ever left your daughter home alone before?" She asked me.

"No...well she lives with her mother, but this was my weekend to have her due to our court arrangement."

"Something I didn't agree to." Melody inserted.

"Melody please." I said clenching my teeth.

"Well, in cases like this where the child is left at home and is injured, we have to step in. And it is in our best interest that the child come with us and be placed into temporary foster care." I could see her lip moving, but the rest of me went numb.

"What?! No you can't take my baby. It....wasn't my fault." I said tearing up.

"I'm sorry, Mr. Logan. That's not up to me; it's up to the judge. Now once the child is discharged, there will be someone here to retrieve her. I'm so sorry. I'll give you two some time to process this." She said and left back out the room.

My mind went completely blank and the room felt like it was spinning. Not to see my daughter? Her smiling face? Her asking me a million questions? Her begging me to go the candy store? This couldn't be real.

"See, I told ya ass. If you would've came back home with us, instead of fucking with that whore, none of this would happen." Melody said not even shedding a tear.

I gave her a cold stare, and suddenly grabbed her ass by her neck.

"Get off of me!" She squealed.

"Bitch, if I find out that you had anything to do with this, I will personally fuckin bury you. Alive!" I said letting her go.

I stormed out the room to go back in my car. I needed to drive around for a moment and think because this shit was too much.

"Manny, what's wrong?"

She said running up behind me grabbing my shoulder. I jerked away from her, still feeling angry.

"This is all your fault, too." I said to her.

"What?"

"If I wasn't so busy trying to show you how sorry I am, I would've been more focused on my daughter."

"Manny-"

"No, stay away from me. All of you." I said and left out the hospital.

I got in my car and drove off.

Maybe I was wrong for blowing up at Bianca when she truly didn't do anything, but right now only thing that mattered was me trying to figure out how to get my little girl back.

18

ZOIENA SULTON

W aking up after what seemed like forever, I looked out the airplane window and seen we was landing at Atlanta International Airport. I was excited about seeing Cash and him showing me around; I've never been to Atlanta before. I got off the plane and went down to the terminal exit where Cash told me to meet him at.

"EXCUSE ME MISS, I'm looking for my girlfriend, have you seen her?" I turn around and see Cash holding a bouquet of red roses.

"OH, I don't know. Maybe she got on the wrong plane and skipped town with her new boyfriend."

"YEAH IGHT, and I'mma fuck her up too." He said handing me the flowers. "Come on. I got the driver waiting for us."

. . .

WE WALKED to his car and got in. Driving for about 45 minutes we made it to this giant castle like mansion.

"Oh my God! This is your house?!" I asked.

"THIS OLD THING? This just for storage ." He joked. We made it up the driveway and the driver helped bring my bags inside.

THIS MANSION WAS HUGE. The ceilings was so high, I prayed for anyone who had to change the lightbulbs. The floors was made of marble and looked like someone shined them on a daily basis. I walked through the hallway and was greeted by a Spanish lady with dark red hair.

"AHOLA, I'm Maria, I am the housekeeper here. I'll be helping you enjoy your stay so anything you need just ask."

"THANK YOU." I said. I looked behind her and seen two cute pit bull dogs running our way. "Aww how cute." I said getting down on one knee and petting them.

"WAIT, you're not afraid of them?" Cash asked me.

"NO. WHY WOULD I BE AFRAID?"

"IT'S JUST most people usually are. I always have to lock them in the backyard when I have guests."

· · ·

"WELL MY DAD use to work as a in-home chef for this lady, and she had two pit-bulls just like these. But they never tried to bite me or nothing. I just grew to love them."

"WELL, that's fucked up. They seem to like you more than me." He said as one of them licked me.

"JEALOUS MUCH." I said pinching his cheek.
    He smiled and reached out for my hand.

"COME ON. I want to show you something." I took his hand and followed him to the backyard, through this pebble stone pathway which lead us to this beautiful garden filled with all different kinds of flowers, and even had a few woodland creatures running around. It was beautiful.

"WOW! WHAT IS THIS PLACE?"

"IT'S where I come sometimes to think. But over here is what I really want to show you."

HE WALKED me over to this white marble headstone. "This is my mother. I had her grave moved here when I bought this place. Cost me a grip, but it was worth it to me. When I come here, I can feel her spirit, her presence. Like she never left."

"WELL NOW SHE knows how much you love her. And that you forgave her for what happened." I said putting my hand on his shoulder.

. . .

"I NEVER BLAMED HER. I was just....hurt that she didn't decide to stay."
He said as I could see a small tear coming out the side of his eye.

"WHY DON'T you try talking to her. Let her know how you feel babe."
He nodded at me and got down on one knee beside the headstone.

"HEY MA. I hope alls well up in heaven...look, I just wanted you to
know...that when you left I was hurt. I was very hurt. But I'm not
anymore." He pulled on my arm to lower me down next to him. "This
here is Zoiena. She's going to be my wife one day." When he said that
I smiled almost crying myself.

We stayed in the garden for a few more minutes and headed back
up to the house. Later that evening, we both got dressed to go out to
this restaurant called *Chama Gaucha*. I wore this two piece short set,
with thigh high boots, and wrapped my hair in a top knot. Cash wore
a Gucci button down with True Religion Jeans. After we bonded over
a nice dinner, he took me for a carriage ride through the park and
through the city.

"THIS IS SO ROMANTIC, babe. Thanks for showing me a nice time." I
said.

"YOU DON'T HAVE to thank me. It's my job to make sure my girl
happy."

"EXACTLY; HAPPY GIRLFRIEND, HAPPY LIFE."

. . .

"ACTUALLY, it's happy wife, happy life." He said pulling out a small ring box. My breathing suddenly stopped. "Look, I know we ain't known each other for long, but Zoiena, I feel like I've known you my whole life. You bring out a side of me that no one has before. When we was sitting in the garden today, the way the light was shining on you was a sign from my mother to me. You're the one."

I COULDN'T HOLD it in anymore, as I started crying because I couldn't believe this was happening.

"WILL you give me the privilege of being my wife?" He asked me.

"YES..YES!" I jumped on him, hugging him and kissing him. He took out the silver 24karat ring and placed it on my finger. This night couldn't get any better.

THE NEXT MORNING, after a long night of us having rounds of husband and wife sex, I woke up to the sunshine on my face. Cash was still sleeping like a baby; I reached for my phone on the nightstand and wondered why I haven't gotten any phone calls or texts. Then I realized I still had my phone on airplane mode. Once I turned it off my phone was ringing nonstop. I had some missed calls from a unknown number that had been calling me for quite some time, but when I picked up they always hung up; I thought nothing of it, and also seen I had a bunch of text messages and phone calls from Bianca telling me to call her right away. I dialed her up and she picked up on the first ring.

"GIRL where the hell have you been? I thought I was going to have to come to Atlanta and find you." She said. I went in the bathroom so our conversation wouldn't wake Cash up.

"SORRY GIRL, I had my phone on airplane mode and forgot to turn it off. But how's things going?"

"NOT GOOD, not good at all. First off Manny's daughter is in the hospital-"

"OH NO, IS SHE OK?"

"SHE'S FINE. Broken arm, but she's ok. But child protective services is going to take her away because they found her alone."

"OH MY GOD." I felt bad for Manny. I knew how much he loved his daughter and losing her was probably the worst he could go through.

"ON TOP OF THAT, he's mad at me, because he thinks it's my fault. I tried calling him but he won't answer." Bianca said sniffling a little bit.

"DON'T WORRY B. He'll come around. You just got to give him some time."

"YEAH I GUESS."

. . .

"So what about things at the shop?"

"Huh? Oh shit! That's what I meant to tell you!" Bianca said. She then went into telling me about Triston building a shrine in his basement, which basically meant he had this obsessive crush on me.

"Are you sure that's what you saw Bianca? I mean this is Triston we are talking about."

"Yes Zoiena, I seen it with my own eyes. Triston is a undercover psychopath. I'm scared to even go to my house or the café since his grandmother told him I came by there. I been staying at a hotel."

This was crazy. I never would've even guessed that Triston liked me, but now it was all staring to make sense why he was always so nice to me. Question now is how do we handle this.

"So what are we going to do?" I asked Bianca.

"I say we call the cops." Said Bianca.

" No....I'll think of something. Just close the café down for a few days and watch your surroundings."

"Ok." We hung up and I opened the bathroom door to find Cash standing. He was listening the whole time.

. . .

"I TOLD you something was wrong with that nigga. I knew something about him wasn't right." He said with this killer look in his eyes.

"CASH, I gotta go back, my friends, they need me." I wasn't suppose to go back until tomorrow morning, but this was an emergency.

"No, Bianca needs you. That nigga needs a psychiatrist."

"EVEN STILL, I think we should both go back. You need to be there for Manny right now."

"YEAH, you right. Ight, well let's at least have breakfast first."

WE HAD a big breakfast that Maria cooked for us, and went upstairs to pack. Once we was ready we got to the airport, and boarded the next flight leaving to LA. We had a small layover in Vegas, so we wouldn't get to LA until 9:00pm.

7 HOURS LATER......

ONCE WE LANDED, I tried calling Bianca but got no answer. Cash was going to see if Manny was ok and drop me off at my house.

"YOU SURE YOU don't want to stay at the crib? I don't feel comfortable leaving you by yourself with that maniac friend of yours on the loose." Cash said.

.　.　.

"I'll be fine. Besides, I do not want to stay at that big ole house by myself anyway." I said.

"Ok, well call me before you go to bed. And make sure all the doors and windows locked."

"Ok, love you." I said kissing him on the cheek.

I got out the car and caught the elevator up to the fourth floor where my condo was. When I opened the door to the pitch black darkness, I flicked the light on and was shocked as hell to see Triston sitting there in my chair.

"Ahhh...Triston, what are you...how...how did you get in here?"

"Doesn't matter. I been waiting for Zo." He said kind of creepy. "Where you been?"

"What..what do you mean? I been with Cash." I said shaking from fear.

"...Zo for a very long time..I've liked you. I've liked you more than a friend. I've liked you more than a sister. I'm in love with you Zoiena Sulton."

"Umm...gee, I don't know what to say."

. . .

HE LOOKED DOWN at my finger that had the ring on it.

"WHAT IS THAT?"

"OH..UM..CASH PROPOSED TO ME." I said nervously.

"WHAT?"

"HE..HE asked me to be his wife."

HE STARTED CHUCKLING TO HIMSELF, reaching in his pocket grabbing a silver revolver. I stood there frozen.

"SO YOU GONNA MARRY THIS NIGGA?" He said holding the gun in his hand.

"TRISTON, PUT THE GUN DOWN...PLEASE" I said backing away.

"No! You gonna marry this nigga Zo?! Why? He ain't nothing but a no good thug, who's gonna break your heart eventually. And then when he does, who you going to come crying to? Huh?!" He said getting up and knocking over my lamp. "You're going to come crying to me. Just like the last time."

I COULDN'T BELIEVE what I was seeing. This wasn't the Triston I knew and loved. This was a monster.

. . .

"Ok, ok...I won't marry him. See look." I said taking the ring off my finger and putting it on the table. "See, just like that. You know you're right Triston; you're absolutely right. I shouldn't marry him, I should be with you. Matter fact why don't you come over here, and kiss me." I said trying to toy with his mind.

"Don't fucking play with me Zoiena." He said now pointing the gun at me.

"I'm not..just come over here and give me a kiss Triston."
    He started to lower the gun and walked over to me slowly. Once he got over to me he had the gun at his side with one hand, and wrapped his other hand around my neck bringing me in for a kiss. I kissed him for a few minutes, before I decided to grab the gun out his hand. He wouldn't let go and pushed me on to the floor, holding my hands down.

"Ya gangsta boyfriend isn't here to save you now is he?" He said leaning down for another kiss.

WHACK!!

Something knocked Triston in the back of his head and he fell over unconscious. It was Cash standing over him with a silver baseball bat in his hand. I got off the floor and hugged him so tight.
    "Oh my god, I was so scared." I said sobbing.

. . .

"It's ok. I'm here." He hugged me tight.

Later that night, the police had come after I called them and said what happened. Cash rather I let him kill Triston, but I just couldn't bare the thought of my friend for so long being killed. Triston was still knocked out, when they put him in the police car.

"Good evening Ms. Sulton, I'm Detective Shar. I just want to assure you that we will be taking Mr. Lester to a holding cell for tonight. He's being charged with two counts of stalking, attempted murder, and assault." He told me.

"Ok, so what happens after that?"

"Well, he will need to see a judge for the final verdict, but most likely they will transfer him to a mental health facility."

"Ok." I said in a sad tone.

"Here's my card. If you have any questions just call me." He said and walked away.

I watched them drive away with Triston in the back seat, wondering why all this had to happen this way. I get in the car with Cash and go back to his house.

The next morning, since the café was closed for a little while, I

decided it was time to go pay my mother a visit. I drove one of Cashmere's cars, since mine was still back at my house and drove to my
mom's house in Riverside. I haven't talked to my mom in months, but
seeing Cash talk to his mom in spirit had inspired me. I got to her two
story house and and knocked on the door.

"Zoiena? Hey baby. It's so nice to see you." She said answering the
door.

"Hey mom." I gave her a hug and went into the house.

"Come on into the living room."

We both sat on the couch in the living room. My mom was really
into old Victorian style furniture, so when you walk into her living
room you would think you was in Buckingham palace.
    "So what do I owe the pleasure of this visit?" She asked.

"I just wanted to see how you was doing."

"I'm doing ok. Me And Curtis just came back from Hawaii last week.
You should've came with us."
    I rolled my eyes at the thought.

"You know you could give Curtis a chance Zoiena. He's not a bad
guy."

. . .

"HE MAY NOT BE, but he's not my daddy either." I gave a fake smile.

"I KNOW he's not your daddy Zo but-"

"YOU KNOW WHAT MOM, I don't want to talk about him." I said trying to change the subject.

"WELL, would you like to talk about the giant rock on your finger?"

"OH....YEAH, WELL I MET SOMEONE." I said smiling.

"OHH. AND WHO IS THIS SOMEONE?"

"HIS NAME IS CASHMERE. He's from Atlanta, and we been dating for a few months-"

"MONTHS?! What do you mean months? You hardly even know this man, and already he's proposing."

"WELL WE LOVE EACH OTHER MOM."

"ZO, I don't think this is love. I think it's his way of tying you down and getting you pregnant, then you're stuck with a baby."

"OH, you mean like dad did you."

She got quiet.

"You know what, I gotta go. This was a mistake." I said getting up and walking out the door.

Sometimes in life people, even your own family, will try and spread negative energy on your happiness just because they're miserable. I was hoping my mom would be happy for me, but I guess I was wrong.

19

MANNY LOGAN

My life turned to hell real quick. I couldn't for the life of me, understand why God was punishing me like this, but I guess he had his reasons. This whole situation wasn't adding up to me. When I got back to the house that night, it was true that Malia was nowhere to be found, which was odd because she's been Naija's nanny since she was born, so for her to just go missing has my brain turning.

Today was the day that Naija was being discharged, after being in the hospital for a week and a half, and my last day to spend time with her before she went away. I pulled up to the hospital and went up to her room. When I got there, she was already woke with some short dark-skin lady sitting next to her.

"Hi, you must be Naija's father. I'm Joan, I'll be transporting Naija today."

"Ok...I brought some of her things. Clothes, and toys, and stuff." I said trying not to bust a tear too early.

"Ok, I'll take them and put them in the car and give you two some alone time." She said taking the bags out my hand.

After she left out I sat on the bed next to her. "Hey baby what you watching?"

"SpongeBob. I don't really like it, but I'm waiting for Dora to come on." This girl loved her some Dora the Explorer. "Daddy do I really have to go with that lady. I want to go home with you."

"Yes you have to go with her. But just for right now, not forever. Then you can come home with me."

"Where's Ms. Bianca?" She asked reminding me I haven't talked to Bianca since the night Naija broke her arm. Now I felt like a asshole.

"Umm...I'm sure she's at home or something."

"Are you guys going to get married?"

"One day."

"Can I be the flower girl?"

"Of course you can."

"Yay." I swear when she was happy it brought me so much joy.

After we watched a few cartoons together, the nurse came in letting me know she was free to go. I helped her get dressed and carried her out to Joan.

"Ok babygirl, you're going to go with Ms. Joan here for a little while. I promise we'll see each other again." I gave her a hug, squeezing her not wanting to let go. I helped her put her seatbelt on, and watched them drive away. It seemed like a part of me left with her.

I got back in my Matte black painted Range Rover, and dialed up Cash on the Bluetooth.

"Yo." He answered.

"Yo wassup, where you at?"

"At The Beverly Center with Zo. We been here for 2 hours just picking out shoes."

I laughed a little bit.

"Hey but how'd everything go, you good?"

"Not really, but I'm holding up ok. This shit is just crazy man."

"Don't stress about it, man. We gonna figure this out and get her back. In the meantime, you should try talking things out with Bianca. Zo said she taking it pretty hard since you blew up at her."

"Yeah I been thinking about doing that. I don't know man. I was just mad, and everything was happening at once. I didn't mean it."

"I told you about that temper of yours nigga. Ever since you was little, you would stay getting into shit."

"Whatever. Just because I'm not soft like you don't mean shit."

"Nigga the only thing soft over here is my girl's ass."

We both laughed. I loved the bond me and my brother had. Most people didn't get along with their siblings, but I did with mine.

"So look, I meant to tell you I seen pops a few week ago." He said.

I instantly got angry.

"When did you see him?"

"Nigga popped up at my house, wanting me to forgive him. I told him he could suck a dick and choke for all I care."

Cashmere hated my dad with a passion. Don't get me wrong, I hated him too, because he killed my mom. I remember that shit like it was yesterday....

14 years ago...

"So you going out for the basketball team or not Manny?" Cash asked me.

"I don't know. I don't think I'm good enough. Everyone taller than me and girls like tall guys." I said as we was walking home together after school.

"Don't let them niggas discourage you. You just as good as they is, and far as the girls, if you hang around ya big bro more often and not them clowns you call friends, you'll get all the hotties you want."

"I really like this one girl. She so fly, I think she goin' join the cheer-leading team."

"Then that's all the more reason to join then, but be careful with them cheerleaders though."

"Why?"

"Because they always end up sleeping with the whole team." We laughed as we made it to our house in the projects. Walking past all the dope dealers and drug addicts, made me determined I was never going to stay in the projects.

We entered our two bedroom, and I plopped down on the couch and turned cartoons on. I loved watching after school cartoons; they had to be the best. Cash went upstairs to look for momma and ask about dinner, while I went in the fridge to look for a snack. Only thing I could find was one fudge pop left in the freezer. We never really had much groceries in the house, until the beginning of the month when momma got her little bit of food stamps the state was giving her.

When I turned around Cash was covered in blood and I was so shocked I dropped my fudge pop on the floor.....

Cash found my mother dead with a gunshot wound to her head. The police came and it was determined my father had killed my mother while we wasn't home, and tried to make it look like a suicide. They tried putting us in foster homes, but we ran away and stayed with one of the homies from the hood. He had us staying in our trap house, which exposed my brother to trapping and getting money. He never wanted me doing any of that stuff and made me focus on school and education. I went to Atlanta Tech University, got a business degree, and moved to California first chance I got.

"Look I know you want to kill the nigga, I do too. But can't we at least talk to him, try to figure out why he did what he did?" I asked.

"If you can find him. Me on the other hand I don't really give a fuck."

"Ight, well I gotta go handle some business, so I'll get up with you later."

"Ight, stay strong little bro."

I hung up the phone and decided it was time I go talk to Bianca.

I head over to her apartment and go up to the fifth floor. I knocked on the door hoping she would be home. The door opened but it was a nigga with a white t-shirt and jeans on that answered.

"Who the fuck are you?" I asked balling up my fists.

"Oh I'm-"

I ain't even let the nigga finish before I punched his ass in the face. Bianca then lost her damn mind having some nigga up in here. I mean yeah we kind of broke up I guess you can say, but it ain't even been a month yet. After I fuck him up, I'm going to fuck her up too.

I started choking the fuck out this nigga until his eyes rolled back.

"Ahhh, Manny what are you doing? Get off of him?" Bianca came out the bedroom trying to stop me.

"No fuck that. How you going to move on to another night and we ain't resolve nothing yet?" I said looking up at her with puppy dog eyes.

"I didn't move on to anyone; that's the fucking maintenance guy. He was just fixing my kitchen sink!"

Rr

I suddenly felt like a ass, and let the guy go. He started gasping for air, and once he caught his breath he got up and ran out the door.

"Thanks a lot Manny; he's probably never going to come fix anything for me ever again. What are you doing here anyway?" She asked. I always thought women looked their sexiest when they're mad at a nigga.

"I came over to apologize. For how I been acting."

"Oh please. You think every time you fuck up you can just say I'm sorry and I'm supposed to go along with it? Well no!"

"Bianca, I know I was a jerk. But you got understand too, a nigga been going through a lot lately."

"So that gave you reason to blame me for your daughter being taken? I am very sad what happened Manny and I want to be there for you, but.....I just can't." She ran back into her bedroom and slammed the door.

I tried opening the door but it was locked. "Bianca open the door."

"No! Get out." She yelled over her crying.

"Bianca please. I'm sorry." She didn't respond. I decided to use my secret weapon, something I normally didn't use, especially when I had to apologize to a girl.

"...if you take your love away, I'll go crazy, I'll go insaaaane...don't leave, don't leave me giiirrrrl, please stay with me toniiiiiiight." I started to serenade her. When I was in my sophomore year of college, I was in the choir for a little while. I always been told I had a nice voice, but I wasn't the type to pursue singing, sign some contract, and get fucked over by one of these music companies.

Once I finished singing "Don't Leave Me" by Blackstreet, Bianca finally opened the door.

"You never told me you could sing."

"I don't like to talk about it much." I said happy she finally let me in.

"…..well don't think you can just sing me out my panties." She said trying to mask her feelings. "You gon' have to do better than that."

"Ok, how about you get dressed and we just go out and chill."

"Fine. But I want to go shopping. All this emotional distress, I'm in need of some retail therapy."

Hours later, after we drove around to 3 different malls, the back of my car was filled with shopping bags. I didn't really mind though. Anything to get back on Bianca's good side, I was willing to do. We went to eat at this restaurant called *Vegas Seafood,* and by the time we left out of there it was dark. But the night was just beginning.

"Manny, where are we going? My house is back the other way."

"Just chill Ight. I got something I want to show you."

"If it's not another Gucci store, I don't want to see it."

"Trust me, this is better than some Gucci purse."

"Uhh, nothing is better than Gucci."

"…what about my dick?" I asked her.

"No comment." She said smiling.

I drove to this quiet street near Santa Monica, in front of this empty storefront with a for lease sign in the window.

"Why are we here?"

"Just get out the car and come on."

We both get out the car as I pull the keys out my pocket to the front door.

"Wait, close your eyes before we go in," I said to Bianca.

"What?...why?" She asked being stubborn.

"Just do it or I'm going to make you stand out here all night." Which I knew she didn't want to do, plus it was freezing out here.

"Ugggh, fine." She said closing her eyes.

I opened the door to the dark store and led her inside.

"Can I open them now?"

"Not yet." I lit two candles and sat them on the counter, next to the little set up I had. "Ok now you can open them."

She opened them and gasped. "Oh my God." She looked at the sign on the wall that read *Bianca's Bake Shop.*

"Manny...is this mine? Is this really mine?" She said crying.

"Yes. It still has some work that needs to be done, but it should be up and running by next week."

"Oh my God, thank you!" She said hugging me.

I picked her up and sat her on the counter behind where the cash register would go. I got a chocolate covered strawberry and put it in her mouth. After she chewed it up, I kissed her on her lips.

"I missed you." I whispered. I kissed her neck, inhaling her perfume that she always wear.

"Mmm." She moaned.

I started feeling on her ass and thighs, then put my hand down her pants and massaged on her pussy. After feeling how wet she was, it made my dick extra hard. I unbuttoned her shorts, and pulled them down her thick thighs. Positioning my head between her legs, I kissed her inner thigh until I got to her middle. Licking and slurping her pussy, it tasted like the sweetest thing I ever put my lips on.

"Ohhh, Manny."

I flicked her tongue across her pearl, feeling her legs starting to shake. With each stroke of my tongue I spread her legs further and further apart, letting her nut in my mouth. She rubbed the back of my head, as I slurped up all her juices. After I was done eating her pussy like some cold pizza, I stood up and unbuckled my pants, pulling my dick out and stroking the tip of it. She hopped down off the counter, got down on her knees and took me into her mouth. Swirling my dick around in her soft, wet mouth had a nigga toes curling.

"Damn, baby. You feel so good." I moaned. She bobbed her head up and down my shaft letting the tip hit the back of her throat.

Eventually, I nutted down her throat and decided now it was really time for me to enjoy her. I laid her back down on the counter and put her legs on my shoulders. Sliding my dick in and feeling how warm she was, had me feeling on top of the world.

"Uhh, shit." She moaned. I sped up faster with nothing but the noise of our skin slapping, being the only noise. Every time we had sex it always felt like the first time, all over again.

As I felt my eruption coming, I went fast making her squirt back to back. If she didn't have a baby in her by now, she was damn sure getting one tonight.

"Aww shit I'm bout to cum. I'm bout to cum." I released inside her, panting trying to catch my breath.

"You know if you get me pregnant, you with me forever right? As in you gon'put a ring on it." She said out of breath.

"Already planned on it. And you know your first cake you make gonna be cum flavored." I said buttoning my pants.

"Why you so nasty?" She laughed.

We got dressed and left out the shop to get back in the car. Even though this day started off fucked up with seeing my daughter go, it turned out good after all.

Woooap! Woaap!

Next thing I know two black cars rode up on us as we was leaving out the shop. Two white cops came up to us.

"Emmanuel Logan?" One of them asked.

"Yes, can I help you?"

"You're under arrest." They turned me around, pushed me up against the car, and started handcuffing me.

"Hey! What the hell for? I ain't do nothing!" I yelled.

"Manny! Let him go!" Bianca yelled trying to get past the two cops.

"Ma'am, please back away."

"Man this is bullshit! I haven't did anything!" I yelled at them when they put me inside the cop car.

"Manny! Manny don't worry. I'm going to call Cash!" I heard Bianca yell through the window.

I don't know why this shit was happening to me. Fuck my life.

20

TRINA MURDOCK

After not hearing from Cash for almost a month, and the altercation from our last visit, I decided to go get some advice from my number one best friend. I parked in front of my mother's house, and used my key to enter.

"MA?!....MA, YOU HERE?" I yelled.

"I'M in the dining room Trina."

I go into the dining room and see her sitting reading the paper and drinking some tea.

"HEY MOM, HOW ARE YOU?"

"I'M FINE. What about you? I haven't heard from you in a while."

. . .

"I'm fine. Junior got an A on his math test, and Brittany took her first ballet lessons." No matter how things may seemed, I did love my kids. I just wish they had a male figure in their life. I wish it was Cash.

"That's good. You ok? You seem kind of down." She asked me.

"Well, you remember that guy I was dating for over a year?"

"The real fine one with all the tattoos? Girl how could I forget."

"Mom!"

"What? I'm just kidding. But what about him?"

"Well, I really like him. Matter fact, I think I'm in love with him. But now he's messing with this other girl, and....I don't know what to do."

"What do you mean? So you got a little competition. So what."

"Yeah, but it's not just a little competition mom. He's been flying to LA to see her every weekend. He buys her presents, takes her on dates...he treated her like a total princess and like I'm nothing to him."

"Sweetheart, if you really love this man, and want to be with him, then you need to up your game a little bit. Begging him to come back isn't going to make him. You have to give him a reason to want to come back to you."

"BUT HOW? I've tried just about everything. I tried popping up at his house, I tried breaking them up-"

"AND SEE that right there is going to do nothing but aggravate him. You have to dazzle him with your wits a little bit."

"...WHAT?"

"I DID IT TO YOUR FATHER." I never heard my mother mention my father.

"MY FATHER?"

"YES. I never told you this but your father was married. To another woman. But by the time I found out about it I was already pregnant with you."

"SO WHAT DID YOU DO?"

"IT'S NOT about what you do; it's about research. Think about it this way, all men have a weakness. You been dating this man for almost a year, and whoever this girl is she's only been dating him for a few months. I guarantee she doesn't know what his weakness is. But you do. And once you figure out how to use it against him, he'll be yours."

.   .   .

I THOUGHT to myself what could possibly be Cashmere's weakness. Then, it hit me like a ton of bricks.

"YOU KNOW WHAT, thanks mom. I gotta go. I'll see you later." I got up and left feeling enlightened. This is why I could literally talk to my mom about anything; she always gave me the answer.

I KNEW Cash had been back in town since yesterday, so I decided to pay him a visit. But before I do, I decided to stop over at Janice house for a little while. I haven't talked to her since my last visit, when she wanted to act like a fucking nun.

I ARRIVE and ring the doorbell but instead of Janice answering the door, it was her husband Jonathan.

"Oh, it's you." I said with an attitude.

"TRINA, HOW ARE YOU?" He said with a smile back. Jonathan was dark chocolate, with wavy hair, and an amazing six-pack. He was standing at the door in some grey sweatpants with no shirt on. I had to admit I was a little bit turned on.

"UMM, IS JANICE HERE?" I asked.

"NAW, she stepped out for a minute. But you more than welcome to wait for her in here."

.   .   .

"WELL, do you know how long she going to be?"

"MIGHT BE A LITTLE WHILE. So instead of you waisting gas coming back over here, why you just don't come in here and wait for her."

"UGGH, FINE." I walked inside and went to sit in the living room.

"CAN I offer you anything to drink?" He asked me.

"I AM THIRSTY. But I'll get it myself; you might try to poison me." I said walking past him to the kitchen.

I GO in the fridge and pour myself a glass of water. As I'm standing there drinking it, Jonathan is just standing there staring at me.

"WHAT?" I asked.

"NOTHING. I just think you're a very beautiful woman." He said.

I STARTED LAUGHING, almost choking on my sip of water. "Umm, aren't you like married? To my best friend."

"I AM. But you know like I know, how your best friend is." He said walking close to me. "Don't get me wrong, I love her and all, but we ain't had sex in months. Some shit about, she trying to focus on finding herself mentally and spiritually and sex will distract her."

. . .

"Haha, Yeah sounds like Janice."

"But I mean she wasn't like that when I met her, you know that. I mean, when we was dating, she was down for anything freaky. We even had sex in a tree one time."

"A tree? How?"

He got closer to me, until my forehead was touching his chest.
"I can show you." He started biting his lip, putting his hand across my breasts, making me feel warm between my legs.

"Uh...I don't know if that's a good idea." I said when he kissed my neck. I wanted to stop him, but for some reason I couldn't.

He put his hand in my shirt and started palming my nipple. He kissed my neck even more making me put my glass of water down. He took my shirt from over my head, making my D cup breasts sit out. I took off my bra from in the front, and we tongue kissed. I don't know exactly what I was doing, but it felt so good right now.

"Wait, what if Janice finds out?" I asked.

"She won't. Nobody has to know." He said lowly.

. . .

HE PICKED me up putting me on the counter, getting in between my legs. Lifting up my skirt, he started playing with my clit. When he pulled his dick out, it was long and thick with a curve in it. Just how I like them. He opened me up, and slid his dick inside.

"OHHHH, SHIT." I screamed. He moved me up and down on his dick, making me cream.

"UGGH, FUCK." He moaned. "Come on my dick; make it nasty for me."

I LOVED the way he was talking. Shoot, Janice was crazy not to hop on this dick every night because I would. I put my legs on his shoulders and leaned further back.

"Mmm, Uhh Uhh fuck me." I yelled reaching my climax.

BEFORE HE COULD REACH HIS, I heard a car pulling up in the driveway. We both froze, and quickly stopped doing what we was doing. I buttoned my bra back up, and put my shirt on, fixing my hair that was now a mess. Jonathan wiped off, pulled his sweat pants up and slipped out the back door.

"Wait, where are you going?" I whispered.

HE DIDN'T ANSWER me and Janice was already coming in the door. I played it cool and pulled out my phone like I was on it.

"HEY TRINA, what are you doing here?"

· · ·

"HEY, you. I was just going to text you and tell you I was here." I said with a fake smile.

"HOW'D you get in here anyway?"

"UMM...THE DOOR WAS OPEN."

"HUH?"

Suddenly, Jonathan come walking through the front door, with earphones in his ear and tennis shoes on. This nigga.

"Hey baby. I didn't know you was back. I just went for a jog." He said kissing her on the cheek.

"HEY. Baby did you leave the door open?"

HE LOOKED at me and then back at her. "Uhh, you know what I probably did. Sorry, won't happen again." He turned and jogged up the stairs. The fact that men was so slick when it came to cheating amazed me sometimes.

I WAS FEELING a little guilty about the fact that I just had sex with my friend husband, but one of the things my mom always taught me was if you not giving your man what he wants, then he definitely going to get it from somewhere else.

"SO LOOK, I came over here to tell you my plan on getting Cash to come back to me." I said.

. . .

"OH MY GOD, Trina, not this again."

"LISTEN, before you shoot me down, I talked to my mother and she helped realize every man has a weakness. And lucky for me I know what Cash weakness is."

"OK....TRINA before you continue, there something I want to tell you." She said with this bad look in her face, that was making my stomach knot.

"WHAT IS IT?" I asked.

SHE LOOKED BEHIND HER, I guess to make sure Jonathan didn't hear her. "Around the time you and Cash broke up, me and Jonathan was having problems. One night after we got into this huge argument, I went out to the bar to let off some steam-"

"OK JANICE, what does this have to do with me?"

"LET ME FINISH. I seen Cash there, and we talked for a bit....had a few drinks....and ended up going to his place and sleeping. Together."

I STOOD there with my mouth tapped wide open. "No...Janice, no!"

"I'M SO SORRY, Trina, I was going to tell you-"

· · ·

"TELL ME WHEN, after my plan works because it's going to work, and me and Cash get married? How could you do this to me?"

"TRINA, trust me, if I could go back and stop it from ever happening I would."

"WELL, you know what too late, bitch. Don't ever call me again." I grabbed my purse off the couch in the living room and and stormed out. I can't believe the nerve of this lying, cheating slut, sleeping with my man. Suddenly, I didn't feel so bad about fucking her husband anymore.

I GOT in my car and before I pulled off I looked up at Janice bedroom window and seen Jonathan in the window. He blew me a kiss, and I gave him the middle finger and drove off.

LATER ON THAT NIGHT, I decided now was the perfect time to put my little plan into action. Zoiena posted on her timeline that she was taking a "baecation" to Atlanta. I guess that mean she was coming here to see Cash, but little did she know she would see more than just him there.

ON MY WAY to his house I got a text from a unknown number.
Unknown:we need to finish what we started....Jonathan

I PRESSED IGNORE MESSAGE, and kept driving. If I was going to get my man back, I needed to stay focused.

· · ·

I ARRIVED to Cash's giant mansion around 10 and punched in the code to the gate pad. When it opened I was shocked, because I thought he would've gotten it changed by now. I guess Ms. Bougie LA had him busy. Well not anymore. Driving up the long driveway , I got to the house and parked. I heard his dogs barking from nearby, but thank God they was on a leash. I hated those things; one time Cash actually sicked them on me.

I KNOCKED on the door and waited. 5 minutes went by and I knocked again. Hearing footsteps, Cash came to the door with his basketball shorts on and a Nike shirt. I could feel my walls fighting already at just the sight of him.

"Trina, what fuck are you doing here? Didn't I tell you to stay away from me."

WITHOUT SAYING ANYTHING, I quickly pulled down his shorts and boxers. He tried grabbing me but I already had his dick in my mouth. See, one thing about Cash is I know he couldn't resist my head. When we was together that's all he mostly wanted, so that's how I knew it was his weakness. Once I felt him stop trying to fight me off, and easing up, I knew I was in. I bobbed my head up and down on his dick so fast my jaws started getting tired.

WHEN HE CAME in my mouth, I wanted to spit it out because I never let him do that before, but desperate times called for desperate measures. I swallowed all of it and unwrapped my mouth from around his dick. I took off my shirt, that I had no bra under, and took off my jean shorts I changed into. I jumped on him wrapping my legs around his waist.

WHEN WE KISSED it felt like old times again. He carried me upstairs and to the bedroom. He laid me down on the bed, ripping my panties off and throwing them across the floor. Before I could even get a feel for it, he slammed his dick into me. It definitely felt like he had grown a few inches since we last had sex, so I was going to enjoy this. He grabbed the side of my hips and was hammering in and out of me, making me squirt all over him.

"Mmmm, fuck!" He grunted going even faster.

I held my mouth open and couldn't even get a moan to come out. I swear Cash had the best dick ever, and it was all mine. Again.

21

ZOIENA SULTON

EARLIER THAT SAME DAY...

I had only seen Cash just yesterday before he flew back to Atlanta, and already I was missing him. Tonight I had a flight leaving to Atlanta to go spend the weekend with him. Now that we was practically married, I was thinking a lot about us moving in together but never bought it up.

I got out the bed and turned on the shower. I just started back sleeping in my apartment after what happened with Triston; matter of fact his court date was today. Maybe I'll go pay him a visit later on today. One thing about Triston is that he could always open up to me, no matter what. While I was waiting for the shower water to get warm, I started feeling a funny feeling. My mouth got watery, and I ran to the toilet and threw up everything, even what I had for dinner last night. This is actually been happening a lot this week. I checked my calendar on my phone and realized I missed my period for this month.

Assuming what I thought, I showered, threw on some clothes, and went to the nearest Pharmacy to buy a pregnancy test. When I got back home, I read the instructions carefully, so I wouldn't mess up, peed on the stick and waited three minutes. After three minutes the stick read positive. At first I felt nervous, but it turned to excitement. Wow, I was really going to be a mom for the first time. I couldn't wait until Cash found out. I decided to wait until I got to Atlanta and I tell him over dinner or something.

I posted on my status "Exciting news, can't wait!" I didn't want anyone knowing just yet, until I went to a doctor. Since I had some time before my flight left, I decided to get the hard part over and visit Triston. They was holding him at a Los Angeles County Jail. I drove one hour and when I arrived, I instantly had butterflies in my stomach. Either I was super nervous or my morning sickness was starting back up. I signed into the visitor log, and waited for them to call me back.

"Zoiena Sulton! You can go back now."

I know it was wrong to come see Triston, after he broke in my apartment and basically tried to kill me, but I just wanted clarification. Before discovering Triston was the monster he was, he was my friend. When I got to the back, they had Triston sitting behind a glass window with a speaker box connected for us to talk through. He just sat there with this cold, blank look on his face, with a beard shadow growing on his face, letting me know he hadn't shaved in a while. I pressed the button on the box, so he could hear me.

"Hey, how are you?" I asked but he didn't respond. He just sat there, staring into space. "...look Triston, I'm sorry how things turned out. I came here today to get your side of the story. What's going through your mind? Why'd you do what you did?"

Still nothing.

"Triston please. Talk to me. You could always talk to me about anything, remember."

Quietness.

I looked at him with this sad look. I didn't recognize this person as my friend Triston. At this point he was a complete stranger to me. When I decided to just leave, I got up from the window and headed for the exit, but then I heard him speak.

"For love." He said.

I froze and then I turned back around, and walked back to the window.

"What did you say?"

"For love. That's why I did it. I loved you Zoiena."

"...why didn't you never tell me Triston? Why didn't you say anything?"

"I...didn't know how. I was afraid, but now I guess I messed up my chances. You're with him now." He said clenching the sides of his jaw.

"I am. I'm sorry Triston. You'll always be my friend, but I love Cashmere. He's amazing, treats me like a queen-"

"I did all of that! I did everything for you, and yet I'm the one sitting in jail!" He outburst.

"You're in jail because you had my face plastered all over your basement like a psychopath, then tried to kill me in my apartment."

"I did everything you would ask me. Even work in that pathetic shop of yours, when I could've did other shit. I devoted my life to you Zoiena."

"Triston, I'm sorry. I wish it didn't have to be this way."

"But it is." He got real quiet and leaned closer to the window. "You know something...I bet he's fucking another girl right now. Yeah, probably not even thinking about ya ass."

"Ok, you know what, guard can you let me out?!" I asked getting up after hearing enough.

"Hey Zo?"

I turned and looked at him.

"I'll be here. Waiting for you." He said with a sinister grin on his face.

The guard opened the door and let me out. It was a mistake coming here and having to hear Triston talk to me that way. It was times where I thought Cash might cheat on me, but something in me just knew he wouldn't. I hope.

I got back in my car, and sat there for a moment trying to recollect what just happened. I heard my phone ding, and seen it was a 911 text from Bianca telling me to come over right away. Anywhere was better than here, so I peeled off to her house. When I got there, I knocked on the door but seen it was unlocked. I opened it to find Bianca on the couch, crying while holding a picture frame of her and Manny.

"B, what happened?"

"Manny's in jail."

"What?! Since when?"

"Since last night. We was coming from my new bake shop and they arrested."

"Well what did they- Wait! Bake shop? What bake shop?"

"Oh…Manny bought me my own bakery. I hope you're not mad," the fact that she was distracted made her crying ease up a little bit.

"No, of course not; congratulations." I hugged her. "You definitely deserve it. Looks like I'm going to need to hire all new staff since Triston is gone too."

"Oh God, don't even mention his ass. I'm glad they put that bastard in jail."

"Yeah for right now. The detective told me that the judge is only going to sentence him to a mental hospital for a year, then probation."

"A year? No that fool need life."

"Yeah…but back to the subject, why did Manny get arrested?"

"I don't know. I went down to the police station and them bitch ass cops wouldn't tell me nothing. I been up all night. I don't know what to do."

"Don't worry, we'll think of something." I immediately texted Cash and told him that Manny was in jail.

"Biiiitch, hold up…is that a ring on your finger?" She asked. With everything going on, I forgot to tell her that Cash proposed to me.

"Oh yeah, I'm an engaged woman now."

"Ahhhhhh! Congrats and you hoe. You should've called and told me. Now I'm not being your maid of honor."

"Aww come on Bianca, please. I'm sorry." Putting on my fake puppy dog face.

"Fine. But you betta make sure you cheat and throw me the bouquet. Because me and Manny is getting married."

"That's actually not the only good news I have." I said smiling.

"Bitch you pregnant too?"

"How'd you know?"

"I'm your best friend. I know everything. How far along are you? Did you tell Cash yet? Is it a boy or a girl? I am the godmother right?" She asked and had me cracking up.

"I don't know yet, no I haven't told Cash yet. I'm going to wait until I see him. Hopefully it's a girl, and yes. You can be my child's crazy godmother."

"I know I am. Who else would be?"

After a while, we made something to eat, watched a movie and next thing I know it was time to go home and pack and head to the airport. I only packed my Louis Vuitton duffle bag, because Cash had bought me a lot of stuff that was already at his house in Atlanta. I drove to LAX, and parked my car in the temporary parking garage. Since I already had my ticket, I didn't need to check in, so I went straight through then TSA line. Once we got boarded I texted Cash and let him know I was boarding the plane and I would be there in the morning. He replied and told me he would have a car waiting to pick me up when I got there. I turned my phone on airplane mode, put my earphone in, and went to sleep.

The next morning....

When I felt the plane land, letting me know we was there, my stomach started getting butterflies again. I wonder if this was what they meant by flutters. When we got to the airport, I stopped at the Starbucks they had inside and got some breakfast. This baby had me eating it seemed like every 20 minutes.

"Zoiena? Zoiena Sulton?" There was a familiar voice behind me, but it wasn't Cash.

I turned around and came face to face with my ex-boyfriend, Derrick.

"Derrick?"

"Hey what are you doing here?"

I wore this unhappy expression on my face, not even looking at him.

"I'm...visiting someone."

"Oh ok, you still live in LA or-"

"You know Derrick, lets just skip the small talk ok. Let's not pretend that we haven't seen each other in over a year, and you up and left me without reason." I finished biting into my sandwich.

"Look....I'm sorry about all that."

"What? Are you serious right now? You put me through hell, and all you can say is sorry?"

"Zo, I....I was in a bad place. I didn't know what I wanted back then."

"Hmm. Well the past is the past so let's move on, and pretend we never saw each other."

"Ok." He pulled out this small card and wrote his number on it. "Listen, if you need anything..I'm only a phone call away. Regardless, I still have feelings for you Zo."

"Mmm, well sorry to burst your bubble player, but I'm taken." I flashed my ring finger in his face.

He nodded his head and walked off. God, the nerve of men sometimes. Like how do you go missing and just pop up at a airport out of nowhere. Feeling disgusted, and a little morning sickness coming on, I decided it was time to go. I went to the terminal exit where Cash said the car was going to be and waited.

I waited for over a hour and a half, and still no sign of the ride. I called Cash phone and got no answer. Suddenly, something started not feeling right. Calling a Uber, and having them come in five minutes, I put in the address to Cash house and was on my way there. He better had a good explanation why he didn't pick up or couldn't answer the phone.

35 minutes later, the Uber was driving up the driveway to Cash house. I got out grabbing my duffle bag and punching in the code on the keypad. I walked in and the house was completely empty. I didn't even see none of the staff. I automatically went upstairs to the master suite and seen the door was cracked open. I go inside, and get the shock of my life.

Cash and some light skinned hoe laid up in the bed naked. I literally thought my heart was breaking as I grabbed my chest. I picked up my duffle bag off the floor and threw it at them.

"What the fu-" Cash instantly woke up and looked around him. He pushed the girl out the bed, waking her up too.

"You lied to me." I said clenching my jaw. "You lied to me!" I turned around to leave. Cash jumped out the bed and came over to me to stop me. "Let me go! Let me go you bastard!"

"No Zo listen to me, this isn't what you think."

"Then what is it?! She accidentally crawled in the wrong bed and sucked the wrong dick?!"

He just sighed. "Zo listen I'm sorry I-"

There was that word again. I released my hands from his grip and slapped the shit out of his lying ass. I took my ring off that he gave me and threw it at him.

"That's all you men are is sorry!" I ran back down the stairs, and out the front of the house. Knowing it would take too long for another Uber to get here, I grabbed the keys to his purple Mercedes-Benz and sped off.

My heart was racing, as I couldn't stop crying uncontrollably. This wasn't supposed to happen; it wasn't supposed to end like this. He was supposed to love and never hurt me. Just like Derrick, I had fallen victim to another man's lies and deceit. Then, on top of that, I was pregnant with his child.

Running a red light that I didn't see, a SUV crashed into the side of the car and I spun around with my foot on the break. After I stopped spinning everything went black.

22

MELODY PRIEST

ONE WEEK AGO....

After pulling my little stunt in the club a few days ago, I thought that would have for sure broken Manny and that bitch up. I guess I was wrong because he still wasn't calling or texting me back. He even told me he was going to refile a petition with the court to get custody of Naija. I couldn't let that happen. While she was over his house again this weekend, I had time to come up with a plan and finally did. It would require me to do something drastic, but at this point I was desperate.

I HAD BEEN WATCHING Manny's house for quite a while, because I knew he would end up leaving at some point without taking Naija with him.

"Do we really have to do this shit sis?" My brother Perris asked me.

"YES, fool. Don't you want to help me get Manny back?" I fired back getting annoyed.

. . .

"Why should I give a fuck if ya baby daddy don't want you? You got pregnant by him, not me."

"Yeah, but I'm your only baby sister. You should be willing to ride for me just like I ride for you."

"Melody, when the last time you done something for me, other than get on my nerves?"

"Ok, so think of this as a one time favor then."

"Naw, fuck that, ya ass too shiesty."

"Uggh, fine...I'll pay you some of the money I get every month for child support."

"Forget it. You can keep that shit. You ain't getting much no way."

I didn't understand why men had to make stuff so difficult.

"I got one better. How about you tell mommy that you really was the one who set the kitchen on fire and not me? Because still to this day she mad about that shit." He said.

"Perris come on; that was when we was kids."

. . .

"So. Do it and we have a deal."

"Fine. Deal."

"Cool. So run by me what exactly we doing again?"

"We're going to wait for Manny to leave, and break into his house. You're going to sneak up on Malia, his nanny and shoot her. Then we're going to take her body, leave it a little way up the road, and leave the rest up to me."

"And how are we supposed to do all this without being seen?"

"It's only going to be Malia and Naija here. Manny gave the rest of his staff the weekend off. He said he didn't want Naija around a bunch of security guards all the time."

"You must really love this nigga don't you? Damn, I hope I don't never make a bitch this dick crazed."

"Shut up!"

We heard a noise, and I cut the headlights down. The gate was opening, as I seen Manny's car pulling out. Without being seen, I quickly drove through the gate before it closed. Parking halfway down the driveway, we both got out the car.

.   .   .

"Ok, look the power supply to the house is around the back. We need to cut the power, and go through the patio door." We start walking up the steep driveway hill and headed around to the backyard.

Finding the power supply box to the house under the porch, Perris pulled out some long pliers and started snipping away. Right away the lights inside the house cut off. Showtime.

I picked the lock to the backdoor, which I was a pro at, and opened the door. I heard voices coming from upstairs in one of the bedrooms.

"Ight, stay down here. This where a man come in at."

"Oh, whatever, just do it and get it over with." I said rolling my eyes.

Perris creeps upstairs with his silencer gun and face mask on. While I waited, I decided to call Manny just to see if he would answer.

"What Melody?" He answered.

"Hey, what are you doing?" I asked trying to sound innocent.

"What do you want?"

"I just wanted to say I'm sorry for the other night. I was drunk and-"

"Mel, save the bullshit. We both know you meant to do that shit. I was just dumb enough to fall into your trap. Now what do you really want?"

"I WANT us to have a good mutual relationship Manny. I want us to be able to co-parent and get along for the sake of Naija. She deserves it."

"I BEEN TRYING to get you to do that for years. Why all the sudden you change your mind?"

"BECAUSE WHETHER YOU believe it or not I love my daughter. And seeing how she lights up around you, I don't want to take that away from her." I decided to play the good parent for now, so that way I wouldn't look like a prime suspect in all this. Even though I was the mastermind.

"OK. WE CAN DO THAT. But one thing you gotta understand is, I'm with Bianca now, Melody. Eventually she is going to be Naija stepmother."

IT PAINED me hearing him say that, but I forgot I was just playing along for right now.
     "Ok, I understand."

"AHHHHHH!" I heard somebody scream.

"WHAT WAS THAT?" Manny asked.

·   ·   ·

"Um..nothing, I'm watching a scary movie. I'll call you back." I quickly hung up the phone.

Perris walked back downstairs, with a black trash bag thrown over his shoulder.

"Did you do it?" I asked.

"Nigga what you think?" He said pointing to the bag.

"Ok, well come on; let's get out of here." I said heading for the door.

Suddenly, I heard some thud noises near the steps, and what sounded like a small cry. I poked my head around the corner to see Naija laying at the bottom of the step and couldn't move.

"Melody, come on, we gotta go!" Perris said.

"Wait, we can't just leave her there."

"Nigga, that's your problem. We gotta go dump this body and go before the cops come. Now let's go!" He said leaving out the back door.

I took one more look at Naija still laying there. I'm assuming by it being pitch dark in here, she tripped and fell down the steps, but I didn't want her to recognize me. I'm pretty sure she was ok, and help would be here soon.

.   .   .

I FOLLOWED Perris back to the car, where he had thrown Malia in the back seat, and he was on the driver's side. I got in, and we drove away from the house. Once we got 2 miles up the road, we stopped and left her body on the other side of the railing. The whole idea was for Manny to get framed for murder, and he of course go to jail. If I couldn't have him, then no one could.

I NEVER BEEN SO happy to finally get home and shower. I still couldn't believe what we just done; it felt so unreal. Hopefully, Naija was ok, and maybe not badly hurt. When I got out the shower, I heard my cell phone ringing and seen it was a number I didn't know.

"Hello?" I answered.

"HELLO IS THIS MS. PRIEST?"

"YES." I said getting nervous.

"HI, I'm calling from the emergency room. We have your daughter here; the paramedics found her home alone at her father's house. Her arm is fractured."

"OH MY GOD. Ok, I'm on my way." I said feeling a little bit concerned.

I HUNG up the phone and went to get dressed. Naija getting hurt wasn't part of the plan, but everything happened for a reason. Only question I had in my head was who called 911?

23

ZOIENA SULTON

B eep....beep...beep
       I opened my eyes to this bright white light, and suddenly felt a surge of pain go through my body. I tried moving but couldn't.

"Oh good, you're awake." The older Black guy said standing over me. "Hi Ms. Sulton, I'm the doctor here in the emergency room. You were in a car accident. You broke your leg, and a few other bones but your vital signs and everything is stable." He said.

Not really remembering what happened, I continued to wince in pain.

"Also, I hate to be the bearer of bad news, but when we took some blood samples, it did show you were 9 week pregnant. I'm so sorry, but the baby didn't make it."

It all started coming back to me. I had just found out I was pregnant yesterday morning, and was excited about telling Cash. Speaking of Cash, I almost forgot about me finding him with that other woman. God, I wanted to die right now. I instantly started crying, not really able to speak because I was in so much pain, physically and emotionally.

"I'll give you some time, but I was just coming to tell you that we already informed your husband. He came in a while ago, and said he was coming back." He said, but I hardly heard him over me crying.

The doctor left out, and I was alone. Not only have I found out Cash was a lying, cheating bitch ass, but that my son or daughter was gone. How could this be happening? I looked at my foot hanging up in the foot sling, wrapped in a giant cast. This can't be happening; it felt like I was in a horrible nightmare and couldn't wake up.

Just then, Cash was walking through the door, and as soon as I seen him, I lost it. I don't know what kind of superhuman, dragon ball z strength came over me, but I jumped out that bed and started attacking him.

"You bastard! You got some fucking nerve!" I started beating him in his head and throwing stuff at him.

"Zo stop! What the fuck? What are you doing?!"

I didn't even care that my leg was hurting so bad; I was focused on getting my anger out.

"You go be with that fucking bitch! Get the fuck out!" I yelled.

Two nurses came in, grabbed me by my arms, and pinned me back on the bed.

"Maybe it's best you leave." One of them said.

"No, I'm not going nowhere." He said.

The nurse then pulled a needle out of her pocket and stuck it in my neck.

After she did that, the room got blurry and I felt really sleepy.

Later that day....

I woke up from the deepest sleep I've probably had, and looked at the window and seen it was dark outside. I looked to the other side of me and seen Cash was sitting there with his head in his hands.

"Why are you here?" I said still feeling loopy off the medication, so I couldn't hardly sit up.

"I wanted to make sure you was ok. I seen the crash, the car was totaled.....also, the doctor told me about the baby."

I started crying all over again.

"Zo, listen. I can't find the words to express how I'm feeling-"

"Then don't. You've done enough. I trusted you Cash. I gave you my heart. I opened myself to you and you betrayed me."

"I know, Zo I....I don't know what happened. She showed up at the door and-"

"I don't want to hear it. Just go, Cash, just leave. We already lost our child, and you lost me. There's no need to be here anymore."

"Zo...please."

"Just go!" I yelled.

He looked at me, and I wanted to really say please stay, but I couldn't. Having two losses in one day felt like when my dad died all over again. Cash got up from kneeling beside my bed, and walked out the door. A part of me wanted him to come back.

I was in the hospital for days, and I didn't even have my cell phone. The nurse said it probably got lost somewhere in the crash. I didn't know Bianca number by heart, so I couldn't call her. Plus, she was all the way in Cali, and I was still in Atlanta.

Knock! Knock!

"Come in." I said.

"Hi, feeling better today." My nurse said coming in.

"A little." I said. Truth is, I been feeling extremely depressed. I wouldn't eat, I refused medications, I just sat here and stared out the window most days.

"Well great news, you're being discharged today. We called your husband and told him he can come pick you up around 3."

"He is not my husband! And I'm not going anywhere with him!" I said crossing my arms. There was no way I was going back to Cash house, and I have to smell the scent of another girl.

"Well, do you maybe have anyone else we can call? If not, we have to send you home with the guy who left us his contact information and insisted on us calling him when you get discharged."

I thought long and hard, and remembered something. I reached for my jeans, and went in the pocket to get Derrick's business card.

That afternoon, I was getting dressed but it was kind of difficult with this cast on. I was trying to put my pants on, but couldn't get it over this leg.

"Struggling, I see?" Said Derrick from the doorway.

"Just come help me."

He walked over to me and helped me get dressed.

"Look, thank you for coming. I…I hope you don't mind."

"I don't. I told you if you need me call me." He said smiling.

Once the nurse got my paperwork finished, Derrick wheeled me out to the car and helped me get inside. The doctor told me it was going to be a while before I could take the cast off, so I was trying to figure out how I was going to catch a plane all the way back to LA and drive with a broken leg.

"You can drop me off at the airport. I'll just catch the next flight leaving to LA." I said.

"Zoiena, you're going to need somebody to look after you while your leg heals." He said.

"I'll be fine Derrick. I don't need a fucking babysitter."

"That's not what I'm saying. What I'm saying is, why don't you just come spend some time at my house until you heal up a little bit more."

"You're joking right. Derrick, we haven't spoken to each other in over a year, and now you want to play captain save a hoe."

"So why'd you call me then?"

"I…I…. I had no one else to call." I admitted.

"Exactly. So it is my job to make sure you heal properly. Besides, I feel like I owe it to you."

"That must be your new dude whose car you crashed." Derrick said.

"No. And he is not my dude. Anymore. How do you know about him anyway?" I asked starting to wish I hadn't called him.

"Well, I overheard a few of the nurses talking. Saying how sexy he was and shit." He said. I rolled my eyes. "Plus, his name rings bells out in these streets."

"Yeah, well I don't want to talk about him." I said looking out the window.

"So does that mean you coming to my house?"

"Uggh. Only because I have nowhere else to go right now, and only if you promise not to try anything funny." I said.

"I promise. I have an extra guest bedroom, so you can crash in there for a while."

After driving for what seemed like forever, we finally reached Derrick's house. It was a cute little three story townhouse with a two car garage. Not as big as Cash house of course.

Derrick helped me out the car, with my crutches and bags, and helped me inside. We entered the kitchen where there was a small room made into a bedroom with a queen sized bed. Well at least I didn't have to climb any stairs. Derrick sat me on the bed and put my crutches up against the wall.

"Well I'm going to let you get settled in. Just let me take a shower and I'll make us some dinner. You still love steak right?" He asked.

"Yeah... hey listen Derrick, I appreciate you letting me stay and all, but this is strictly all it is. Once my leg feels better, I'm going back home to LA." I said so he could get an understanding.

"I get it, Zoiena. But can I just say one thing?" He asked.

"What?"

"It sure is good seeing you again." He said smiling and left out the room closing the door.

I laid back on the bed sighing, looking up at the ceiling. How did I get myself into this?

24

CASHMERE LOGAN

"What the fuck do you mean she's gone?!" I shouted at the secretary.

"I'M SORRY SIR, but she was already discharged this morning." She said back to me.

"No, fuck that. I'm not trying to hear that shit! I told y'all to call me when she was ready to leave."

"WELL IT SAYS HERE that she requested for the nurse not to call."

WHEN I HEARD THAT, I felt so angry I could feel steam coming out my ears. I instantly grabbed my cell phone and dialed Zoiena's phone but it went straight to voicemail. Zoiena couldn't have left out of here by herself all bruised up with a broken leg. So if she didn't leave out of here by herself, then who did she leave with?

TRYING TO CONTROL MY ANGER, I dialed up Dex, my own personal computer whiz and hacker.

"Yo whaddup?" He answered.

"DEX, I need a favor. I'm at Memorial, can you look at the cameras and see if you can see if Zoiena left with anyone?"

"SURE. I can actually do that in about five minutes, hold on for a second."

I HELD on the phone and waited for him to do his thing. Zo had every right to be mad, but I was still responsible for her, and she needed to just hear a nigga out.

"GOT IT. Looks like she left around 10:30 this morning, and some guy is helping her to the car."

"CAN YOU GET A FACIAL RECOGNITION?" I asked getting anxious.

"NOT REALLY. The video is kind of blurry, but she got into a 2019 Lexus, which is registered to a Talia Pearson. She lives at 329 Kingston Ave."

I SCRATCHED MY HEAD, now this shit really wasn't making sense.

. . .

"IGHT THANKS DEX." I said. Why the fuck would a nigga be picking up my girl? I don't know but I was damn sure going to find out.

I GOT BACK in my car and drove straight to the address Dex gave me. The shit was way on the other side of town, but I got there in no time because I drove fast. When I got in front of the house, I walked up to the door and started banging on the door.

"YES, CAN I HELP YOU?" A cute light skin girl answered the door. She kind of reminded me of Ayshea Curry.

I DIDN'T SAY ANYTHING. I brushed past her, walking in the house.

"HEY! What the hell? Who are you?! You can't just come up in here!"

I IGNORED HER, and went up the stairs. She had three bedrooms, and I checked all of them and the bathrooms. I came back downstairs, and seen her dialing 911 on the phone.

"YES HELLO? Yes there's someone-"

I GRABBED the phone out her hand and slammed it down. She looked at me with fear in her eyes.

"WHERE IS SHE?" I asked.

. . .

"Where is who?"

"Where is my girlfriend?"

"How am I supposed to know?" She said.

"So your name not Talia Pearson?"

"Yes. But Pearson isn't my maiden name. I'm divorced."

"And you don't own a 2019 Lexus? All black?" I asked.

"I use too. After the divorced, my ex-husband took everything. The house, the car, half my bank account. I had to start all over." She said.

Something still wasn't adding up. Why the hell would Zoiena be with this bitch husband?

"Do you know where he is?" I asked.

"I wish. But no. So can you get out my house now?"

I grabbed her up by her arm.

. . .

"THIS WHAT'S GOING to happen. You're going to find out where your bitch ass ex-husband is, and you're going to call me and tell me." I took her cellphone from her pocket and dialed my number.

"AS SOON AS you find out, hit my cell phone. And if I find out you hiding anything from me, you're going to regret it." I let her go and left out the house.

DRIVING HOME a nigga felt so lost. Not only have I lost my fiancé, but my unborn child that I didn't even know about. Fuck, why did a nigga have to slip up. I don't know what came over me. All I know is Trina was at my doorstep, and before I could tell her to get the fuck on, she started sucking a nigga dick and next thing I knew my knees buckled and dick got hard as cement....

THE OTHER NIGHT....

I WAS on the phone with Manny, trying to figure out what the fuck happened and why he was in jail.

"So they not telling you anything, bro?" I asked on the phone.

"NAW, saying I should know why I'm here, but I don't. I know I ain't slipped up on my child support payment, so I don't know what the fuck is going on." He said back.

"DAMN. Well don't worry. We gon' get you out. I'm gon' hit up Bernard, that Jewish lawyer and fly him out there to handle this shit."

"*Thanks bro. Hey, could you do me a favor?*" He asked.

"Wᴀssᴜᴘ?"

"I ʙᴏᴜɢʜᴛ Naija a teddy with a spy cam in it. Could you just check on her and see how she's doing?"

"Iɢʜᴛ I ɢᴏᴛ ʏᴏᴜ ʙʀᴏ. Keep ya head up in there. And don't drop the soap nigga." I joked.

"Fᴜᴄᴋ ʏᴏᴜ." He said hanging up.

I ᴡᴇɴᴛ to my laptop and went to the live cam that was linked to Naija's teddy bear. When it came up, it showed she was in a bedroom by herself, with a bookshelf, toys, and her own bed. This shit look a lot nicer than some foster homes I seen. She was sound asleep, in her twin sized bed, with her legs and arms sprawled everywhere. It was fucked up she had to be in this situation, but it wouldn't last long.

"Sʟᴇᴇᴘ ᴛɪɢʜᴛ sʜᴏʀᴛʏ." I said closing the laptop.

Sᴜᴅᴅᴇɴʟʏ, I heard a knock at the door. It was late at night, so whoever this was definitely wanted to get fucked up. I went downstairs and opened the door to see Trina standing there.

"Tʀɪɴᴀ ᴡʜᴀᴛ ᴀʀᴇ you doing here? Didn't I tell you stay the fuck away from me?" I said getting ready to slam the door in her face.

. . .

BEFORE I COULD, she jumped on me and started grabbing at my basketball short.

"What the fuck? Get off of me!" I yelled.

I TRIED MOVING her hands and pushing her away, but my dick was already in her mouth. Shit. She started making my shit feel so wet. I don't know what came over me, but she was building up my urge to nut. She went fast as a bitch going up and down with her mouth. When I came down her throat I was surprised she swallowed it. I would always try to get her to swallow, and she would never do it, just spit it out. When she got up off the floor, she got naked down to her underwear, and pulled me upstairs.

WE GOT TO THE BEDROOM, and I pushed her down on the bed and started ripping her bra and panties off. I don't know why I couldn't stop, but my dick was doing the thinking at the moment. I guess that was where I fucked up.

I slammed my dick inside her wet ass pussy and forgot how tight she was.

"OHH YES!" She screamed. "Fuck me Cash. I missed this dick."

I WENT FASTER and faster and turned her over and started fucking her doggy style. Seeing her ass bounce on my dick, just gave me even more motivation to keep going on. I held her head down with one hand and squeezed her ass with the other.

"FUCK TRINA. Why you gotta do this shit to me?"

. . .

"*Because I love you. I love you so much.*"

I didn't even hear when she said that, because I was already cumming.

"*Uggghhhaahh, shit!*" *I'm came on her back, and passed out after that.*

The next morning...

The next morning, I woke up to something heavy hitting me in my face. I wake up and see Zo standing there and seen Trina laying next to me. I quickly pushed her ass out the bed and jumped up. What hell just happened?

"*You lied to me.*" *Zoiena said clenching her face.*

"*No Zo, listen to me, this isn't what you think.*" *I said trying to stop her from leaving.*

"*Then What is it?! She accidentally crawled in the wrong bed and sucked the wrong dick?!*" *She yelled.*

"*Zo listen, I'm sorry I-*" *Before I could finish, she slapped the shit out of me.*

"*That's all you men are is sorry!*" *She said and ran back downstairs.*

. . .

I RUBBED my hands over my head, and turned and seen Trina still smiling. I went in my closet and grabbed my mini play pistol, and started shooting at her.

"HEY...STOP... WHAT THE FUCK CASH?!" She said hopping around like a monkey.

"GET THE FUCK OUT!" I said, then I heard a screeching noise outside. Looked out the window, I seen Zo driving away in my purple Benz going down the driveway.

"WHEN I GET BACK, you better be gone." I said with a stern look to Trina. I quickly got my clothes on, and went outside, hopped in my Ferrari and drove after her.

DRIVING at at least 80 mph, I tried my best to catch up to Zoiena. When I got 4 miles down, people were standing all in the middle of the street. I honked the horn for them to move, but they didn't. I got out the car to see what was going on and seen my purple Benz and a black truck had collided with each other. I pushed through the crowd, thinking the worst has happened.

"Zo! Zo!" I yelled.

I GOT to the car and opened the driver's side door. Her head was up against the steering wheel, and she was bleeding everywhere. I pulled her out making sure to be carful with her body. I laid her down on the ground trying to wake her up.

. . .

"Zo! Zoiena! Come on please! Please wake up!" I shook her face but she didn't respond. "Come on baby please. I'm sorry. I'm sorry for what I did.. Please, please don't leave me like this."

WHEN THE AMBULANCE *got there and told me where they was taking her, I got in my car and did something a nigga never did before. I prayed. If I lost Zoiena, I would never be the same. Ever.*

I GOT TO THE HOSPITAL, *the same time the ambulance did, and they took her straight back to surgery. Sitting in the waiting room feeling helpless, I called Bianca to let her know what was going on.*

*"*FAMILY FOR ZOIENA SULTON?*" The doctor came out and said.*

*"*ME, I'M HER HUSBAND.*" I said standing up.*

*"*HI, *I'm the ER doctor on staff today. So the surgery went well. She's pretty bruised up with a fractured leg, but she'll be just fine."*

I WAS RELIEVED *to hear that.*

*"*THERE'S ALSO *something you should be aware about. We did some blood-work and it turns out that Ms. Sulton was nine weeks pregnant."*

MY RELIEF WENT TO SHOCK. *Pregnant? Why didn't she tell me?*

. . .

"I TAKE YOU DIDN'T KNOW?" The doctor asked.

"NO, I didn't. Is the baby going to be ok?"

"I'M SORRY. We did everything we could. But the fetus did not make it."

MY HEART SUNK to the bottom of my stomach. I always wondered would it would be like to be a father since mine wasn't never in my life, and when I had the chance I lost it all at once.

"WE'RE GOING to be transferring her in a bit to a regular room. But you can go in and see her when you're ready."

NODDING my head I went outside. I needed a minute alone.

I GOT INSIDE MY CAR, and just lost it. I never really cried about shit, but this shit here hit home for real. I promised Zoiena I would never hurt her. On top of that I lost a child I would never get to hold. I banged on my steering wheel, and sat there and cried for about a hour. There's got to be a way to fix this...

WHEN I GOT HOME LATER that night, I laid straight on my brand new bed. I automatically ordered a new one, after what happened because I didn't want to smell another woman on my sheet. I wanted Zo. I'm glad that she was ok, but angry that she ran off with another nigga. Even though I probably deserved it, Zoiena was mine.

.   .   .

My phone started ringing and I answered.
"Hello?" I answered.

"Hey, it's Talia."

"You got some info for me?"

"I do. I know where they are."

TO BE CONTINUED.......

SUBSCRIBE

Text Shan to 22828 to stay up to date with new releases, sneak
peeks, contest, and more....

SUBMISSIONS

To submit your manuscript to Shan Presents, please send the first three chapters and synopsis to submissions@shanpresents.com

CPSIA information can be obtained
at www.ICGtesting.com
Printed in the USA
LVHW090726210619
621865LV00003BB/441/P